NELLIE WITHOUT HUGO

ALSO BY JANET HOBHOUSE

JANET HOBHOUSE

Nellie Without Hugo

Anchor Books
DOUBLEDAY
New York   London   Toronto   Sydney   Auckland

AN ANCHOR BOOK
PUBLISHED BY DOUBLEDAY
a division of Bantam Doubleday Dell Publishing Group, Inc.
666 Fifth Avenue, New York, New York 10103

ANCHOR BOOKS, DOUBLEDAY, and the portrayal of an anchor
are trademarks of Doubleday, a division of Bantam Doubleday Dell
Publishing Group, Inc.

Nellie Without Hugo was originally published in hardcover by
The Viking Press in 1982. The Anchor Books edition is
published by arrangement with the author.

Library of Congress Cataloging-in-Publication Data

Hobhouse, Janet, 1948–1991
Nellie without Hugo/Janet Hobhouse.—1st Anchor Books ed.
p. cm.
I. Title.
[PS3558.O3369N4 1993]
813'.54—dc20   92-5532
CIP

For Mouse,
with love

NELLIE WITHOUT HUGO

I T SEEMED TO NELLIE that life was as deforming as an ill-fitting shoe, and that by a series of small, forced adjustments—the slow, world-wise business of surrendering natural edges and boundaries—she had become a strangely shaped creature. Increasingly in her thirtieth year she felt that something was not right. Yet she was not Madeleine, for whom a Miss Clavell could turn on the light and re-right the grotesque appearances and terrors of the night, and she had no switch to bring back the sweet order of day. Instead, the permanent world of wakefulness in a dark, silent room, and no procedure to deal with it; instead a dread that became, she thought, an eagerness to give away something in herself to attain harmony in, and a sense of rightness about, that world.

If she thought about other lives—that of her grand-mother, say, or of some long-dead artist—she was tempted to see there some presently lacking order. On the other hand, she suspected that the lives of the dead seem clear only because they are dead, and may be reduced, as in a *Times* obituary, to salient facts: birth, trials, successes, wives, wealth, health, death. While alive it was conceivable that grandmothers and painters bumped around in their nights, bruised their shins, cried out against the darkness, listened to their hearts pounding under blankets, prayed for morning, stunned themselves with drink, told fairy tales to bring on oblivion, or sweated in their shirts alone with their own secret fears in precisely the same manner as herself.

And yet they may have lived, as she lived, in a world that called itself a daylit, simple world, as bland as Bloomingdale's, as accessible as the 42nd Street Library, a world whose doings could be accounted for by simple narrative or its shorthand—UPI tapes, Wall Street reports, doctors' findings—a world on which you had only to lift the shades and name what you saw and there you could be, in the world, with the lights on and everyone smiling.

At that moment Nellie was lying with one leg stretched out on the sofa, the other leg on the floor, a position conveying simultaneously an invertebrate contentment and a readiness to run. What Nellie thought she was expressing was a temporary collapse, brought on by the nervous strains and necessary dissimulations of her farewell to her husband, just now on his way to the airport for a seven-week trip to Africa, leaving with Nellie a space in their life together that must be filled by her life alone. And it felt really, a bit threateningly, like a small blank canvas, a piece of pristine future, an opportunity and a bottomless pit, into which any amount of sensation and deed might stumble and fall.

Now that Hugo had gone, there was a strange quality to the silence inside the room, as though the quiet were a kind of matter that had come to fill the vacuum where Hugo had been. It was odd the way the walls boomed with stillness and the things in the room—desk, vase, flowers and cat—were beginning to look "realer," cer-

2

tainly more material than five minutes ago when Hugo had been stirring the air and breaking the lines of sight, creating shadows and setting up static with the motion and liveliness of his departure. In that sudden lull, it was as though all the chairs and the tables, the cushions and books had taken a deep inhalation of air, and come themselves to their stout and weighty life. As though, with Hugo gone, they were presenting themselves as populace enough for Nellie's world.

Normally the objects that Nellie lived with depended sadly on her power to infuse them with existence. There was no problem making the facing sofa disappear, one had only to think of something else, of Hugo say, or of work tomorrow. The more constant problem was to allow the sofa, now hallowed by evening light, chosen and cherished by sleeping cat, covered by Nellie's papers and color transparencies, to have its due, its chintz-bearing existence. For that to happen a thing had to be noticed, named and stepped-aside for. And all of that was not normally easy.

If Nellie had been a painter she would have been happy to go about like Adam in his nameless universe, pointing and calling at this thing and that until a world existed, personally verified, for which she, like Adam before the distractions of Eve, could be center, chief observer and recorder, praiser in an endless journey through a world of things. She would not have been an abstract painter she thought—when she thought about it at all, when the miscellaneous properties of objects did not interfere with her pure sight of them: the state of their relation to her, whether underfoot or out of reach, immoveable or in disrepair. Even now it would not be long before a sofa that received the evening light along with the weight of the

3

cat and Nellie's papers would find itself defrocked, profaned, become an object simply to be tidied. One acted on things, normally, or else, as in the case of the papers sitting there to be read, of the cat sitting there needing dinner, things acted on one, so that one had from time to time to adapt oneself inside the world, renounce the power of Adam before the Fall and settle for the democratic push and shove of the modern relation of a person to things.

Nellie put the leg that had been comfortably resting among the sofa cushions on to the floor, turned her body and stood up inside the apartment, ready for the first bit of ritual necessary to repossess the formerly shared habitat. The adopted procedure was similar to, though a reversal of, what she had once seen in a film about the hippopotamus, whose habit it was to make territorial claims by dropping turds at the boundaries of each new homesite. She had been moved by, she had almost been sympathetic to, the frailness of identity of these indisputably solid creatures for whom, nonetheless, the world was not to be relied upon until it had been staked out by solemn excretions to the East, West, North and South. Thus was made a safe self-smelling place in a dangerous wilderness, full of hippopotamic terrors: the lion, perhaps, and the crocodile, famine, disease, all the possible annihilations of the riverhorse's world.

So now Nellie, in similar spirit, went through the apartment, removing all signs of a previous existence, picking up ashtrays, straightening cushions, replacing books, resetting her stage for a future one-person show, though not without a little guilt, so that in the bedroom she could not quite bring herself to change the sheets, so clearly an act of repossession did it seem. She would do it

4

tomorrow when it might be done more neutrally, or when, to be honest, the sensations of conscience would be weaker.

Instead, she picked up two pairs of Hugo's socks from where they'd rolled off the bed while he'd packed his suitcase, and put them in the now-devastated sock drawer, lingering a bit to note the space in the drawer and to run her finger over the edges inside for signs of lint and loosened tacks. As her arm went up to turn on the light with the dangling switch she noted for the third time that day that she must fix the switch, that the screwdriver was only across the hall in the kitchen and it would take precisely two minutes, and then for the third time that day she promptly forgot as soon as her fingers left the switch and her head turned where the light directed her inside the room.

Only in this room did there remain the signs of the winter move, trunks used as end tables on either side of the bed, the television on the floor, papers and books stacked in one corner, waiting for Hugo's construction of shelves, waiting rather in vain. By unspoken agreement Hugo and Nellie had conspired to leave this room unfinished, to postpone a statement of character, here, at least, at the central site of their joint living. Here, as nowhere else in the apartment, were empty walls and bare floors, an absence of settings and—with the sole exception of the flowered shelf-paper that Nellie had fitted the first morning after their move—final touches. Here alone had they managed both to preserve the illusion of transience and to avoid naming the nature of their fantasies and the nature of their habits. Unlike the rest of the apartment, this room had a vague, yet not a hotel-anonymous identity, being neither Nellie's place—marked by her taste in pictures or fabric, nor Hugo's place—a reliquary of his bachelorhood. Instead it was, as is proper for scenes of sexual victory and sexual strife, a no-man's land.

There was a hum inside this room and a faint sound of Germans shouting. At first Nellie noted that the bedroom walls were finally, as long suspected, showing themselves thin, but listening again, she located the source in the clock radio that must have been singing into space since eight o'clock that morning. Nellie increased the volume and waited until she recognized a sprechgersang from Mozart's *Seraglio*. Accompanied by this she pulled the sheets and covers over the bed, despite the fact that she would be inside them within a few hours, and then undermined her own sense of order by stretching out on the new-made bed the better to enjoy the Mozart and the pleasant gradual body sensations of being without Hugo.

A pack of cigarettes and matches from the restaurant last night lay in a chipped ashtray on one of the trunks—thus far and no further did their bedside hedonism extend. Nellie would have liked a drink but was too content and too conscious of the precariousness of that state to get one. Instead she lit a cigarette and smoked in bed, watching the smoke drift towards the ceiling in time to the music. Though the music ought to have called forth a vision of hookahs and little sweet cakes on a brass platter, of total ease and recline, what appeared now to Nellie as she smoked was the gray-striped image of a burnt mattress, black-gouged and hauled out on the street among cat-peed newspapers and empty cartons. In New York, you did see these terrible blasted and abandoned beds rather often; hard not to wonder what could possibly have become of their inhabitants, dozing off with cigarettes and waking later inside a wall of flames. Wasn't there a seventeenth-century priest who, having fallen asleep on his deathbed, woke to find the flames licking about him. "What," he cried, "not already!" But perhaps it was the association of smoking with sex that made bed such a good place for it. Well, there was that old joke, too, about smoking, after. Stupid.

From where she lay on the bed, in imagination still rocking slightly in the wake and chop of Hugo's departure, Nellie could see the long corridor that led to the kitchen and the living-room. Through the open double doors of that large room she could sense its pleasing formality, now faintly lit by the May evening light, all its lines running parallel or perpendicular, sofa backs or window frames, table legs and baseboards. That room was cool and orderly and colorful. Mozart would not have minded living there, alone, mind, not with Nellie. When Nellie and Hugo were there together the place seemed crowded and disorderly, though Nellie was by nature tidy and though by New York standards the flat was too big for two people. Nellie's sister Rebecca had predicted they would rattle about the place like dried peas in a pod, but actually no apartment could contain the swells and tempests of married life and like every other place they'd lived in, this apartment when they were loving was unnecessarily large, and when they were not, threatened hourly to crack at the seams.

The physical difference made by two, not one, was peculiar. Even now Nellie had a sensation of cooling and contracting like some fallen meteorite. The molecules that made up herself seemed now to be rushing towards her center, propelled by the heat lost in Hugo's disappearance. She felt distinctly smaller and denser, as though when Hugo was there her being and his joined and swirled among the expanding gases. Perhaps that did explain all the eruptions and explosions of two people together: it was the molecules rubbing shoulders, locking horns.

Nellie's thoughts began to scuttle into corners. There was a small scratching panic about the evening ahead, a fear of passing it alone with the cat and the nameless dreads as the sky would darken outside, and one by one lights would be lit like hurricane lamps against the possibilities of night. And in the other direction was a tappy shuffling of pleasure that this and some fifty nights were to be hers for the having. And then over all this too was her wonder and irritability at the predictability of these responses and a sense that she and Hugo were perhaps trapped rather than merely described by the rhythm of this mechanism—the protected lone heroism which they both enjoyed in separation and the swing back to a furry togetherness that let them function in the world, get on with their work, their friendships, their marriage. It was their contract. If the price of this peace was loss of lust, of ambition, a blunting of spiritual and emotional life, at least they both connived at it, made it a fraternity of weakness in which each loved the other because each was forgiven.

And besides, what else was going? Other marriages, other couplings were, weren't they, once past the blinding stage, tales of weakness, tales of woe? Perhaps settling for such friendship as she and Hugo had was stoically correct, perhaps it really was the small part not to be thrown away with the detritus of married life, nor counted among the

8

miseries of arguments, the mindlessness of property, the failures of morale, of sex, of heart, the airlessness of living with another whose every mood affects your own, who like the weather presses in on everything, beating down, rain or shine, filling up the sky, charging the air, defining the day.

Well, Nellie had wanted to be alone, and now she was alone, and, already, realizing that, she thought she felt a tender anxiety about Hugo. Today Hugo had been a little removed, grateful for the free life to come and solicitous for Nellie for the coming separation. He was himself clearly not altogether easy about the journey, not the work part for the book was going well, but the moving part, which though he dreamed of constant travel, he never really liked. The flying made him nervous and in the strange sterile hotel rooms he hardly slept. But such discomfort forced him to seek companionship and his loneliness made him real to himself. When he returned he always felt stronger, happier, a more solid part of the world.

For Hugo connection with the world was a business of activity and, literally, transportation. If Tanzania did not exist for him, as it did not for Nellie, to whom newspaper reports seemed as much a fiction, a literary convention, as a seventeenth-century masque, the act of hurtling himself through the skies on to foreign soil did what the unaided imagination could not do, convinced him of its reality. Once Hugo had visited a place, it never ceased to have existence for him, and he, by association, became real too, blessed by its materiality, situated and geographically accountable. Hugo was part of the world every time he traveled in it, each contact with its foreignness made him

9

more familiar to himself, so that the more he left home the more at home he felt.

But for Nellie, being somewhere was no guarantee of anything. Traveling made her anxious precisely because she felt the "real self" left behind. Visits to friends that in New York had been anticipated pleasures became in the moment hopeless failures to conquer jet lag, boredom, strange food, short funds and other petty surprises, together with the disappointment that no one sits still in life the way they do in imagination.

Nellie moved the cat off her feet and got up to stand by the large window looking out on to the street below. There was little movement under the streetlamps, one or two cabs passed slowly and a police patrol car. In the apartment block across the way two parties were going underneath an old couple in a kitchen eating supper. In one, Nellie could see people her own age sitting on the floor, smoking, drinking, perhaps listening to records, rather slouched mostly, sullenly waiting for later sex, presently hanging out. The other one was like a Christmas party, with children and grannies dressed up and staying out late, with guests moving in and out of rooms carrying plates and glasses and bowls of colored ice cream. But it felt pathetic to be staring out like that. Nellie pulled down the blinds. There was nowhere for her to go at this hour, except eventually to bed. And since that was where she was bound to be she began now to undress, though it was still early. Under the covers she listened to the noise of the elevators that came between the spaces of the nearly ended Mozart and reached to switch out the light. Then she lay quietly and thought of Hugo in his plane, saw him upright with his book in his hand and his third drink on the little plastic tray in front of him, saw the plane gliding through the night clouds, carrying him away from her at that terribly slow, dreadful speed of transatlantic jets.

From the outside it appeared that Nellie's future had been settled by her marriage to Hugo. Certainly her mother regarded the wedding as the light-hearted conclusion to Nellie's few years of wildness. "Wildness" was hardly the appropriate term for Nellie's confused carryings-on, but compared with the narrow and happy correctness of her childhood, for which her mother had been quietly grateful, it was a term that would serve. That brief era apart, and it was, after all, the early seventies when Nellie was sowing oats, and when by all accounts things might have been worse, it had long been clear to Nellie's friends and family and often to herself—hence, perhaps, the premarital shying, the mild revolt—what sort of things she would be doing, what sort of people, clothes, reading, there would be, the moderateness of the pain of her life, the number of its pleasures. That predictability of ease had arisen naturally from the received assessment of Nellie's needs and nature, her long-accepted role within the family —the sane one, the least trouble, the happy and self-sufficient child, industrious—at times to the point of dullness —gratifyingly reliable.

Until the age of seventeen when Louisa had married again and taken the family to England, Nellie had been brought up with her two sisters in a large dark-walled apartment overlooking the park. In those days it seemed that the dust on the parquet rose constantly at the slap of her mother's boa-covered slippers as they crossed and recrossed, leading the dogs, in response to this crisis or

11

that—a disaster at school with Sara, a tantrum from Rebecca, some erotic misadventure, some brandished threat to domestic peace. And it seemed to Nellie that her childhood had been passed in refuge from such crises, off in her little room with her stuffed bears, her paper dolls, her French grammars, her Henry James, while the storms and humiliations of female life boomed and creaked about her.

Even now, over Nellie's remembrance of her girlhood there hovered images of her mother in love. Of her mother replacing the black telephone receiver in its cradle, eyes shining with politics or pleasure. "Well, you won't guess who that was," she would announce to whichever of her daughters was home from school, chastely uniformed and importuned to act as Mama's confidante. Or passing her daughter in the hallway, pretending to hide her tears, or if her tears were not in that gloaming hidden, snuffling gently and protesting, "Nothing, it's nothing, get on with your homework." Or of Mama answering the door to some new-lauded beau, her long strides billowing her silk skirts, the air stirring with her perfume, a moment's intake of breath, a last half-second of theater and conspiracy with her girls before the door was swung open in greeting, and the demure and triumphant smile would appear.

And the depressions, long listless evenings when things were going badly and Louisa would be eager for her daughters' company, for talk of school and films and books —for the happy pretense that they were all girls together.

Yet Nellie saw in her mother's life no old-fashioned romanticism nor any touching virtue, but something obsessive and unfree, and as she grew older vowed not to appear such a fool, to herself at least, in such matters. More than this, it seemed to Nellie that lurking behind all Louisa's old-fashioned busyness with the comings and goings of her lovers was a simple panic passed on to her daughters, a panic of being left alone—a certainty of the uselessness of the unalleviated female life. None of this was expressed, of course. In outward manner and conversation Louisa acknowledged the superiority of women and of the independent life. But that life was a kind of heaven which only saints attained, devoutly to be wished of course, but in the meantime . . . And so she pursued it —love, at first in its most glamorous, later in less ambitious, form, and in the frequency of her conquests began to see for herself a kind of success. And quantitatively measured, there could be no doubt, Nellie's mother Louisa had been loved.

At the end of the opera Nellie reached out to turn off the radio and peered into the silent darkness. She was wide awake. For several minutes she lay still and tried to determine whether the movements in the dark were real or imaginary. Then she got out of bed and crossed the corridor towards the kitchen. Naked, in that unlit apartment, she felt more vulnerable to intrusion, yet she left the darkest areas of the apartment dark, unwilling to provoke her cowardice by acknowledging it. She allowed herself only the light of the refrigerator in the kitchen, keeping the door open with one foot while she poured milk with some difficulty into a glass. Knowing, in the manner of those nineteenth-century British explorers who dressed for dinner in the African bush, that it is attention to the details of civilization that keeps chaos at bay, Nellie refused to drink straight from the carton.

The light that threw its arc above the butter dish and

yoghurt containers reached beyond the white wall telephone to the cork billboard that with less theatrical lighting might not have been noticed at all, so full of asterisks and arrows and conflicting signals of urgency had it been. Now, however, Nellie could see, among the out-of-date gallery notices, the much-underlined reminders of bills, and a now-useless, once-frantic note to Hugo to pick up his shirts before—as Nellie suspected—they might be pulped along with other quarterly detritus of the Chinese laundry, was tacked a postcard from Nellie's sister Sara. On the side of the card that faced Nellie where she stood drinking milk and leaning against the refrigerator was a picture of an odalisque by Matisse, the painting owned by a museum in California where Sara now lived.

The lady on the postcard lay among a large number of pillows and stared out at Nellie in confidence, not only of her eternal desirability—she of the pantaloons and gold bracelets, her French rather than Algerian features adorned by a striped turban, her bare feet spangled and stretched out upon a rough hassock—but in confidence too, and pleasure, that nothing could enter that realm of silks and velvets and embroidered wools to disturb her luxurious calm. For though it was possible, looking at the odalisque, to imagine a first moment of intrusion, a slipping of silk over skin, the touch of gold and hair and cloth, it did not seem to Nellie to be a picture about seduction, but rather its opposite, a picture about the distance there was between the painter and what he painted. For the space that allowed Matisse to paint his odalisque (observe her) was also the space that kept them apart. He could see and record as long as he did not possess. Any closing of the gap, and the vision would disintegrate. In fact, the closer

Matisse came to his subject, the more blurry (and abstract) it would have to become.

Nellie reached out and took the postcard off the board. On the other side of the card, in rather abrupt contrast to the mood of the painting, was Sara's message to Nellie:

Life terrible at the moment, must say. Ricky awful. Hope you two OK. May well be seeing you soon. How are you? Miss you all. Will phone.

All love,

Sara

The style of the note, telegram-like, boded ill, as though a great deal more than pronouns was being left out. Whenever Sara wrote like that, chopping out her Is in brutal self-effacement, and wavering violently between private cry and social banter, it was clear that something in Sara's life had gone amiss, and that Sara was sorry—in advance—for the trouble this was bound to make. But then that had been that. Nellie had phoned several times to California in the weeks that the card had been around and then had rather forgotten it, in the spirit traditionally adopted with Sara of no news being good news, of sleeping dogs and so on. A month ago Sara's message had been hung on the corkboard where it had remained until now successfully hidden beneath the bloomers of the nesting vamp.

Now among the cushions and rugs of the lady Nellie once more had the image of Sara, prone of course, in the eternally repeating mode. That posture it seemed had always been—the childhood flu spells that kept her whole winters out of school and the collapses at college when Nellie had sat on the edge of Sara's bed holding Sara's hand mid-afternoon as the shouts of the sporting set came in through the windows, and Nellie would say, "Oh come on, Sara, it's not as bad as that." Sara would reply that Nellie knew nothing about it because she wasn't Sara, but always added, "Thanks for coming, please forgive me," saying that Nellie should leave her alone and not worry; it wasn't Nellie's fault that Sara was a mess, etc. Or Sara back from hospital or vacation or a failed affair, back in, or on, or headed towards her bed at home, while Louisa paced and fretted audibly outside her door.

Different memories of that adolescence, but in each of them, Sara was flat and Nellie upright, Sara was whimpering and Nellie was silent, Sara was silent and Nellie was arguing, but the one was always down and the other always up, straight man and fall guy, the perpendicular Hollanders. Until Sara's engagement to Ricky nearly two years ago, just after the last of Sara's Caribbean recuperations, and then after the engagement and almost unexpected, the miracle marriage, when for weeks the family had walked around not daring to breathe, teeth gritted and fingers crossed like gnarled roots, like figures on some Expressionist relief poster.

And then Sara had gone away to California and managed for the last year and a half almost to have been forgotten by her family, so relieved were they, Nellie, Rebecca and Louisa, by the absence of bad news, of the sight of the frail body, stricken once more, confined to bed, by what was simply, even possibly for others enviably, Sara's life.

And yet there it had been all the time, silenced by the din and thump of Nellie's life with Hugo, only now audi-

16

ble, the statement of disaster, weeks old but with its own nasty freshness nonetheless.

Nellie picked up the phone and dialed the number of Sara and Ricky's house in Beverly Hills. It would be seven-thirty there, time to change after tennis, rinse off the chlorine or get out the coke spoons for the evening ahead, a likely time to reach Sara.

The phone rang sharp and cheerlessly twelve times into the Californian air. Then Nellie replaced the receiver, took her foot from the refrigerator door and faced the intervening darkness between herself and her bed.

LOUISA SAT in the morning light of the large living-room window and filed her nails with a long metal file. It was her birthday, and today she was sixty. She would sit and wait for the flowers and phone calls and try not to panic. After all, nothing had changed. It was simply her birthday as yesterday had been the day before her birthday and tomorrow would be the day after. Yes, but yesterday she had been fifty-nine and thus, legally, linguistically in her fifties, tomorrow she would be in her sixties. Thus today she would age a decade. The thought alone was enough to give her gray hair.

She must try not to cry. She had cried on her fiftieth birthday, but that had been an exceptionally difficult and disappointing year, just before the divorce with Jack and all that scandal about Sara at school. She had cried, too, the day she became thirty, at the imagined loss of her power over men, but that had certainly been premature, because since then—well, no point counting and gloating. If only she'd been able to tell her thirty-year-old self, indeed her fifty-year-old self, that there was nothing to dread, been able to speak out of the future, out of this chair, out of this body, with its same (more or less) hip size, been able to whisper from this morning across those years to that series of fearful women who'd all had birthdays on this day, to say, "Don't cry, Louisa, I guarantee it will be all right." Well, perhaps out there ten years hence was a figure with blue-rinsed hair (Louisa shuddered) trying to stage whisper, *"Courage,* my dear, you'll get by."

Yes, but what if out there was nothing but disease and loneliness and gradually failing strength, what then? Louisa had spent such little time thinking of mortality, she was *so* unprepared. Perhaps she ought to have set aside an hour a week, among the lunches and facials, and like a seventeenth-century prelate taken out the alien skull. "When I behold" and all that. Instead, she'd frittered her life away in the pursuit of—what? What had she got? She would go empty-handed to the grave.

Yes, well, she said, brushing the parings from her lap, how else to go? And, really, what grave? She was only this side of menopause, not even a grandmother yet. Bless her daughters, not one had made her a grandmother.

Louisa got up from her chair and began to pad across the floor towards the clock. It was ten, why hadn't there been a call? Sara was on California time, but Nellie and Rebecca? Surely they would not forget. Louisa took out her checkbook from the drawer of the desk under the clock. It would calm her nerves to pay some bills and add up sums on her little pearlized calculator, a gift from Harry. She very much liked paying bills and doing accounts. It gave her a sense of where she was and in what state of health, financially of course, but these things spilled over into other areas. It certainly soothed her nerves to know that she could pay her phone bill and her credit card accounts and still have money to spare. Wealth conferred a sense of margin, of time yet, time and space before the squeeze—whatever that would be.

You knew where you were with numbers; they accounted for a great deal. Quite right that in the Middle Ages they had been credited with mystic powers. There was certainly something very chaste and purifying in balancing a checkbook, getting the sums to come out right. But the peculiar thing was that numbers didn't stand still, but shifted around rather. For example, sixty dollars was not a large bill to pay American Express, yet sixty was a large number of years, not as bad as eighty, but still. It was funny that after your twenties you figured your age on a scale of thirty-five, forty perhaps, whereas with bills you figured on a hundred. Everything over a hundred is probably expensive, and everything over forty is probably old. Only that wasn't true either because Louisa hadn't been old at forty. Sara had been six and Louisa had been her young(ish) and quite beautiful Mommy.

Poor little Sara, so bad at games and so competitive. Louisa had continued to learn the rules of countless games just in order to encourage her daughter, long after it was clearly hopeless. Nellie was so impatient with her and Rebecca was already in college—No, not yet, Louisa said, that was her last year as an ugly dumpling, before the swanning. How she hates her graduation photo! Well, Louisa always told her to be patient, that it would come in its own time—life and loves—and of course it did, or will soon. There you are, you see, everyone has a different time. For Rebecca her teens were pure hell, where for Louisa . . . well, for Louisa as she was then they were the high point of life, yes, and in some respects it was never so wonderful again.

Fancy surviving so many feelings and still having them (in more moderate form, of course, thank God). An incredible heart. And the rest, apparently. Eberhardt says in excellent shape. But compared to what, one wonders? Old Eberhardt is ten years older than Louisa himself, perhaps he makes allowances. Or perhaps he merely means that she has kept her figure whereas a good many women her age . . . well, no need to go on. Disgusting how they let themselves expand as though to take up more room in the universe now that they're about to leave it. No thank you, Louisa has always had a large enough piece of life without herself needing more than her allotted space. No worry, she will not be overlooked. Although she does find it distressing not to be able to command the same admiration in streets and restaurants. There used to be a time she almost had to cover her face like Muslim—or is it Hindu?—women in order to get across town. But how nice, and how it kept the stride going, knowing that in every step of one's long, beautiful leg, another potential suitor was calculating his odds for making one's acquaintance. Well, one must admit things have changed, though in restaurants still, with careful lighting, one can yet detect some of the old predatory fervor among the male diners. Nothing more depressing than the way they otherwise continue with their meals as though nothing but a fly had entered the room. Louisa has felt remorse at her failure to compete with a bowl of soup.

Still, she has had her day and can be content with that. And she has Jack occasionally when he's over, and Harry —why hasn't he phoned? And there's poor William on the horizon—though that's a little distressing, and perhaps she ought to stop it now before he gets hurt. Still, waste not, want not. And the girls. Perhaps Rebecca is in court this morning. That must be it. Louisa has never seen

21

her in court. Would it be amusing to watch Rebecca harangue the judge and jury? Probably not, probably rather like Rebecca with Harry when she was sixteen and he was drinking. Little Carrie Nation, she used to call her. But she could be *so* tiresome, and lowering, like a storm cloud crossing the prairie, and poor Harry would sit there lolling about, trying to keep his good humor and getting more and more depressed as Rebecca went on at him, and he not able to get out of his seat for fear of looking foolish, and therefore trapped, like that poor boxed-in jury. And come to that, Rebecca rather likes a drink herself these days. One has noticed. There you are, you see. Things really do change with age, things sort of get better. One's grip on life is not so deadly. You let go a bit. You get gayer, *faute de mieux.*

Louisa licked some stamps and pressed them on to the envelopes for the bills. Then she made a neat little stack in the corner of her desk, put away her checkbook and eyed the telephone. She knew that if she concentrated hard on the phone it would ring, but she did not want that. She wanted her callers to act of their own accord. The sight of the black phone at that proximity, regarded with that urgency, pleasingly reminded her of her former triumphs, when by erotic magic she could force the precious sound from the inanimacy, connecting by such means with the voices that had dominated her days. Deep, controlled male voices like Harry's or tender, almost vibrato, excited voices like Jack's, with its to her unfailingly distinguished British accent. Perhaps she had even married Jack because of that voice and what it promised of another world, a world that when she got there seemed so bafflingly taken up with horses and dogs, china tea sets, gin and golf. And those headscarves that British country women wore day and night, shopping and at point-to-points, as though every one had some scalp disease or scurvy under the chin? And when Jack presented Louisa with an undoubtedly expensive square of silk (with saddles and belts printed in lavender) she thought it was a joke. He was crestfallen, poor angel, wanted so to make her an English lady, and there she stayed, pining for the city lights and the feel of solid, solid concrete underfoot. Those walks in the English countryside, with ferocious Minis and Porsches bearing down on one just around the next hedge, and cows everywhere in the road, filthy with cow excrement and wet all spring and all winter, and God knows, most of the summer with that relentless British weather. Yes, it did her complexion good, but her hair frizzed up. Eventually there was a pied-à-terre in London, quite nice in a poky sort of way, though Louisa did so loathe the carpeting and the smells of English dinners in the corridor: brussels sprouts, generally, and gray beef with jelly! You couldn't get decent vegetables anywhere except Harrods. Louisa remembers how embarrassed Jack was when she told the women about the veg and fruit market at Harrods. Hypocrites! Always pretending to be poor, always boasting about bargains and saving used envelopes.

Louisa walked over to the window that looked out on to Central Park. From the sixth floor the trees were large and green and looked fluffy. The reservoir sparkled in the sun. On her left she could see the buildings of the Metropolitan Museum and the blocks of stone that had been, as it seemed, forgotten in construction and left piled on the roof. The gods on the top of the museum were black and dirty, theologically accurate, as Jack said. Around the reservoir were runners and dogs and an occasional horse and rider. Louisa opened the window and tried to smell the park, but she could not. Instead she listened to the long-suffering sound of the buses as the air-brakes went on and off, the sounds of the car horns and the occasional pedestrian shout. She loved Fifth Avenue in the eighties more than any other part of the city, more than the Village where Rebecca lived or the West Side where Hugo and Nellie lived. She loved the color of the stone houses that led off the avenue and the breadth of the street that seemed on days like today to collect all the sun and all the energy of the city and send it round and round the shimmering reservoir, or collect it in whirlpools around the museum steps and the entrances to the park, bottlenecks of mothers and babies, young elegant males with expensive dogs, and on the weekends, divorced daddies with their baseball-pajamaed sons.

She loved the sounds of the city when you opened the window and the way they differed from the sounds inside the apartment. Inside and outside were different kinds of life that you only heard from an upper-story window. Going out *on* the street, mingling with the crowd, was another matter, invariably disappointing and, of course, potentially hazardous. *Pace* Jack and his promise for the English hills, the park was all the greenery, all the botanic seduction Louisa needed. Just the sight of those brave, soot-choked boughs, those patches of as yet untrodden green, was all the pastoral her heart could bear. How foolish and unnecessary ever to have left New York.

Well, at last, the phone was ringing. She must try not to sound cross.

24

"Hello?" she asked.

"Hello, Mama."

"Yes, darling, who is this?"

"Sara, Mama."

"Sara? Darling, it's so early for you. You shouldn't have gotten up so early. I could have waited."

"It's all right. I haven't slept. I'm coming to New York today."

"But how wonderful. What a lovely surprise."

"I've got to get out. I'll be there around nine tonight."

"Sara, what is it?"

"It's so hot here."

"Hot?"

"Yes, and Ricky's gone."

"Gone?"

"Yes, he's away and he comes back tonight. I don't want to see him."

"Why not? Oh I see, you mean a row? Darling, you must expect the first years of marriage . . . Oh I see. No, darling, you must stay where you are. Ricky will be so unhappy to find you gone when he gets back."

"It doesn't matter to Ricky. He doesn't care anymore."

"Well of course he does, my darling, we all care."

"Mama, please."

"Yes, of course. Now what time do you say?"

"The plane gets in at nine."

"Good. Right. Well, see you then."

"Thank you, Mama."

"It's all right, darling."

Louisa's first thought was that it was wrong that this should be happening on her birthday. Then she wondered how she would get Sara's room ready at such short notice. Last, she remembered that Harry was coming to take her to dinner tonight and that Sara would have arrived in God knows what state and it might upset him. She must put Harry off or change the dinner to a lunch, but could Harry do it at an hour's notice? Of course not, and now she would have no fêting at all on her birthday. She must call Nellie. Nellie could always deal with Sara, but would she come? Damn, what was wrong with Sara, always coming to grief and landing her messes on other people's door-ways? No, of course it was all right, just that at sixty one did not expect to have to be picking up after one's children's lives. Certainly not still, and especially not on one's birthday.

ON THE EVENING of Sara's arrival, Harry was not around. Nellie was there, fixing her mother and herself drinks in the kitchen, breaking the ice in the trays against the stainless steel sink.

"Do you have to make that terrible noise, darling? The ice comes out perfectly easily if you pull the lever. Can't you see it?"

"I like to get it out this way," Nellie answered.

"Suit yourself." Louisa had ceased to argue with Nellie some ten years ago. She now went off towards the hall, in response to the sound of hesitant shuffling by the door and the noise of the elevator descending.

Louisa opened the door, forgetting to look through the peephole, and saw Sara carrying a large, heavy case with a broken zipper. She was tanned and rather dirty around the mouth, as though she'd been sucking candy all the way in a small, open plane.

"Hello, my darling," said her mother, "how healthy you look." Stepping backwards into the hall, she called to Nellie that Sara had arrived.

Sara stood on the threshold, her head faintly bowed. She was half a foot taller than her mother, a fact which Louisa forgot whenever she was gone and resented each time she reappeared. "Come in, darling," she said reaching up to

27

embrace her, just a little awkwardly so that it became necessary to say, "Now, where will you put your bag? Just here I think." She indicated the door of the hall closet, but then remembering that her daughter's room was ready, made a sign to Sara of mock-senility and pointed down the hallway. "So silly," she said.

Sara took one long step inside the apartment and dragged her case behind her. "It's so nice in here," she said shyly.

"Oh no," said Louisa, "we have to be painted again next month; I've just let it go and let it go. It hasn't been done since before your wedding."

"Yes," said Sara.

Nellie came along the corridor from the kitchen carrying two glasses of Scotch, one of which she handed to her mother. She did not kiss Sara, but said hello with a childish formality, and asked her what she wanted to drink.

"Whatever you're having, thanks," Sara said, "but can I just go in here first?" Sara slipped past them and went into the small bathroom. She felt sick still and unhappy and now uncertain whether it had been a good idea to come. She thought she could feel Nellie and her mother exchanging glances. She was making difficulties. Also, she felt foolish in front of Nellie, whom she had not expected to see, felt as she had when a young girl and something had happened at school. Nellie would say, "Tell, Sara, come on, tell or I'll tell."

Sara made sure the door of the bathroom was locked and then braced herself against the sink. She turned on both taps and looked at herself in the mirror. Her eyes looked dark and unhappy, yet rather beautiful, wide, well-shaped, black-brown, like the eyes of film stars. She wondered why Ricky hadn't noticed that her eyes were beautiful, especially since she had been so unhappy. Sara watched her eyes in the mirror until she lost all sense of ownership or connection, but was able to take from them the encouragement and sympathy they seemed to be offering. It was what she had come here for, and it did not make much difference whether the sympathetic gaze came from that reflection or from the two women waiting outside. Calmed, she regarded her brown hands as they hung under the shiny ropes of water that came from the fish-shaped taps. Then she bent her head and washed her face with her hands until a pink showed under the tan and the edges of her hair were wet. Not having a comb, and not wanting to walk out in front of her mother to unzip her bag, Sara pulled at her hair with her fingers. It would have to do, and because it would have to do, she did not now appraise it in the mirror, but breathed in, shallowly, quickly, and opened the bathroom door, turning out the bathroom light as she re-entered the hallway and moved towards the low noise that came from the big room.

"Better, darling?" asked her mother.

Sara nodded. Behind Louisa, where she sat on the large white sofa near the window, the lights across the park seemed all to be on.

"Well, here I am." Sara smiled lamely and folded herself opposite her mother into the dark green armchair.

There was a silence among them in which the sound of ice against glass rang clear and provocative. Nellie watched quietly while Louisa projected like an old character actress the sympathetic mother. Sara did not know how to start, and really was rather moved by the sight of all those New York windows lit like a constellation of hanging stars, like the show at the Planetarium where Louisa had sometimes taken Nellie and Sara when they were younger. Then, all the stars was all there was, filling up the view, nothing but those little points in the pitch that you could look at for hours while a soothing voice-over told you what you were seeing, what it all meant, for hours until the ugly auditorium lights went on again and everyone readjusted, blinking and self-conscious.

And now they were all waiting.

"Well," said Sara. It was so pathetic having to tell, such a defeat. "I am here and Ricky is there, that's all really."

"All?" said Louisa. "But what's happened? Now, come on, Sara. What has happened?" Louisa sat forward on the sofa trying to convey both an earnest sympathy and a mother's anxiety, but the expression was tainted, it seemed to Nellie, with a little bit of simple curiosity.

Sara looked down into her lap. She felt silly sitting in Louisa's rather formal living-room in her tee-shirt and jeans, like a child home from playschool. "Ricky's in love with someone else," said Sara, "that's all."

"You mean he's left you?" asked Louisa in horror.

Sara looked over to Nellie, where there was nothing but attention, as usual, as though Sara were "behaving," instead of simply telling something, and with difficulty. "He hasn't left, no," she said to Louisa. "He comes home; he's home now. No, he's probably with her, not at home."

"Who is she?" asked Nellie.

"I don't know."

"Oh my poor baby," said Louisa, returning to the response appropriate to the first announcement, "but if he hasn't left I think you should be home waiting for him." She had tried to disguise it, but her voice conveyed disap-

30

pointment in the size of Sara's revelation. "It will pass," she said. "These things do happen. Especially, I should have thought, in California."

"Do they," Sara looked towards her, "happen in California? I didn't know."

"Oh don't be silly," Nellie said. "Hollywood is full of all that stuff, isn't it? That's what it's famous for, isn't it? It's Ricky's line of work."

"I didn't know," Sara said, depressed.

"Well, you didn't teach her much," Nellie said to her mother.

"Nellie, Sara is very upset." Louisa turned to Sara, "You'll get over it, darling. It happens to all of us, and we've all survived."

"How did you?" said Sara, looking at Nellie. "How did you survive, Nellie? How did you get over it?"

Nellie was now uncomfortably caught between them. "Actually," she said, "it hasn't happened to me. As far as I know."

Sara turned a questioning face towards her mother. "Well, it isn't a *guarantee* in marriage," Louisa said, trying to laugh. It came out a sort of gurgle. "But of course," she said with renewed cheer, "it does happen, and women learn to deal with it. If you love someone you overlook such things. I know it's hard, but you can't just end a perfectly wonderful marriage because Ricky has momentarily strayed."

Sara looked damp and depressed.

"It's not practical," said Louisa finally.

Nellie got up and offered Sara a cigarette. She took one, but sat still as Nellie got the matches and then she smoked unhappily, like someone being punished.

31

"How do you know it's 'perfectly wonderful'?" Nellie asked Louisa.

"Well of course it is," Louisa said. They were now both talking as though Sara were no longer present.

Sara, sitting back in the armchair in an unhappy smoke-clouded slump, leaned forward and said, "Look, I'm really sorry you think I'm making too much of this, not being grown up, all that. I can't help it." Her breath and talking and smoking were all going in and coming out in bumps and jerks. "It's not a question of thought and deciding to do this or that. The pain just doesn't go away. I don't sleep. It's just there."

"Well, of course," said Louisa looking towards Nellie.

"And everything has changed," said Sara.

"Now, Sara," said her mother, "nothing has really changed. Ricky is still Ricky. Only your feelings have changed, and I am absolutely certain that after a little time away it won't seem so terrible. That is all that is needed, just a little time." Louisa smiled again, as though she'd handled something well, an intractable servant, a mad dog, an unblooming flower. "For the moment we'd all adore to have you here, but you mustn't make things worse, aggravate them."

"Aggravate?" said Nellie. "Things couldn't be any worse, as far as Sara feels them. Don't you see that?"

Sara was now listening to none of this, but steadily smoking her cigarette, sitting back in the large chair, trying to finish it without dropping too much ash.

Louisa did not like this competition with Nellie. "Nellie," she said, "I have been through two divorces and several near-marriages and I tell you categorically that things

32

could be much worse. You don't give up a good man without a good fight."

"How can you use such horrible language?" asked Nellie.

Louisa continued, "It is simply her pride that has been hurt; she will survive."

"I don't think so," said Sara. Nellie and Louisa looked at her.

"I don't think it's my pride," she said simply. "You don't understand," she said to them both. "This makes everything different. Ricky is not himself any more. I am no longer me."

"Oh," said Louisa. And then, "That will pass, my darling, I promise you."

"No," Sara said, "it's all too late."

Sara had now finished her cigarette and seemed tormented by finding an ashtray.

"Well it's just over then," said Nellie, pushing the crystal shell towards her. Nellie spoke to Sara in the language of their teenage infatuations. It made a kind of alliance between them, a premise of youth with its infinite future against Louisa and her notions of squeeze, security, holding fast to that little that there was.

"I don't understand at all," Louisa said now, vexed as much by the display of age-loyalty as by the logic of Sara's despair.

"Well, there's not too much to understand," said Sara, no longer in this language of youthful squander, but in some other manner, her voice cracking a little, but whether from tiredness or the approach of tears you couldn't say. "He's gone."

33

Louisa fiddled in her pockets for a Kleenex, found one and handed it to Sara. "Here, darling. He'll be back," she said, "be patient."

"You don't understand," Sara said. Though her child's voice played Louisa's game, it was clear that the conversation was over.

"No," Louisa said, "I don't suppose I do." She let the words betray her vexation. After all, it was the evening of her unnoted birthday. Nellie had not even seen Jack's beautiful flowers on the table in front of her, the little note still crisp among the petals. From where she was sitting, not noticing anything but Sara, she could practically have read it: "Many, many more, darling Louisa."

"Sara," Nellie said, "perhaps you should go to sleep now. Aren't you tired?"

"Yes." Obediently, Sara got up from her chair. Then she began slowly and ludicrously to shake. The shake started at her shoulders like a flapper's dance and went through Sara's legs. Louisa was embarrassed. "Sara, darling, you're shaking," she said. "Nellie, give Sara some brandy."

"No . . ." Sara said, "I'll go to bed, don't worry."

"It must be the temperature change," said Louisa. "California must be so hot. Nellie, darling, close the window."

"No . . . I'll go to bed . . . I'll be better tomorrow . . . sorry."

But Sara did not move. She remained towering above her mother and sister and the huge bowl of flowers on the table, shaking and breathing quickly. She did not cry and she did not look at either of the women. Finally, she turned her head towards the hall and with the weakest show of will managed to get herself out, away, free from the scrutiny of the women who had not been where she had been and were not where she was now.

AT THE BAR of the Sherry Netherland on the Monday after Sara's return, Nellie sat waiting for Rebecca. She had meant to speak to her before, principally about Sara, but Rebecca had been very busy with some case and, Nellie supposed, with her new lover, the psychiatrist Robert, and Nellie had been busy with her museum work and the absence of Hugo. Tonight, since she was having dinner with an old friend and Rebecca was meeting Robert downtown, they had decided to meet here, a place convenient to both offices, good for cabs, and despite the hookers, both exotic and pedestrian in clientele. The sisters had met here often before, after work and before dinner, for the pleasure of sitting at the bar and watching the unattached out-of-towners watch them for signs of possible commerce, while yet protected by the character of the bar as a perfectly respectable, if somewhat luxurious, meeting-place for ladies. Tonight, however, having changed at the office into what she hoped was a flattering black silk dress, Nellie was more vulnerable than she wished to male misreadings. She kept her eyes firmly fixed on the dish of peanuts in front of her and made do, as innocently as possible, with Perrier and lime.

Only ten minutes late, Rebecca pushed in through the glass doors, raising hopes and toppling umbrellas as she made her way to where Nellie sat, head down among the drinkers. She had that wonderful tired Rebecca look, after the ravages of her office day, and just before the ravages of her night with Robert. There would be a bath in between and new makeup, but Rebecca's disarray rather suited her, as now when half-shut briefcase in hand, old raincoat titillatingly open on bare brown throat and the full curve of Rebecca's bosom, she sat in fluster of greeting with Nellie. If Alex, Rebecca's partner at law, weren't so totally unaware of what went on around him, Rebecca might be dressing like lady lawyers elsewhere, man-tailored suits and colored pantyhose. As it was, Rebecca didn't look like she could defend anyone, defenseless rather, but perhaps that was how it was done. "Nellie," said Rebecca, pushing away the hair that had fallen from its pins and hung dampened by the small spring rain. She looked around her at the bar, straining the top button of her silk blouse and netting several smiles, "you are still safe, I see."

Rebecca hoisted her old leather bag on to her lap and rummaged inside for her cigarettes and lighter. "Whiskey sour," she said to the bartender, and to Nellie, "God, what a day. Well?"

"Well. First, thank you for Tuesday, and letting me finally meet Robert." Rebecca waited, but Nellie went on. "Sara came back Thursday, not very happy."

"What's Ricky done?"

"It's hard to tell how serious he means it to be. There's someone else. Anyway, to Sara the thing is over."

"Oh," said Rebecca, "oh God. What does Louisa think?"

"When I was there, Sara had just arrived, Louisa was trying to get her to go back, or think about going back."

"Do you think she will?"

"No."

"Do you think it's going to be bad?"

"It's impossible to tell. But you go and see her."

"Oh I will, of course, and I want to bring Robert."

"For Sara?"

"Don't be silly. For Mother. They ought to meet." Rebecca waited for what Nellie ought to be saying next. In the silence she ate peanuts.

"He's very nice, Robert," Nellie said.

"Yes, isn't he?" Rebecca was inordinately cheerful.

"Is it very serious between you two then?"

"Not sure," said Rebecca. She had a sudden maternal shyness now. She sipped her drink. "He's a wonderful lover," she said, "very kind and very sexy."

"God," Nellie said, "you don't really think like that do you, Rebecca? Like an advertisement."

"Don't be so sharp, Nellie. You married women ought to be more tolerant." She ate the orange from her cocktail.

"Oh, by definition," said Nellie, "we are."

"You really ought to try single life again before you start scrutinizing single women or their terminology," Rebecca said. "I'm sorry to say, these things end up being important, sex and so on. Sorry to shock you. He's a wonderful lover," Rebecca said obstinately, "he really is."

It was possible Rebecca was simply boasting, or trying to impress Nellie in an area she imagined impressible, Nellie wasn't sure. For a while she sat and watched her sister's face as Rebecca fumbled once more for a light. There was no self-consciousness in it, and no tautness either. It seemed loose, as though slipping down towards Rebecca's lap. If it fell Nellie would see the old Rebecca, surely, the sixteen-year-old solemn scholar for whom all the important things of the world could be put inside the large ink-marked school bag, smelling so powerfully of old leather and pencil shavings, holding the notebooks in which Rebecca wrote, pressing down hard on the lined paper with her schoolgirl intensity, and the paperback poetry books, all underlined, the margins full of exhortations and salutations to the writers, responses and thank yous, and the noisy declaration of her feelings. And now Rebecca seemed sort of shaken loose by her life since then, all those many years since she was sixteen and getting As in everything.

"Rebecca?"

Rebecca came up out of her bag with her lighter. By her face it was clear she had already forgiven Nellie her remarks about Robert. Nellie was like that, after all.

"What?" she said.

"Rebecca, do you think you're going to get married?"

"To Robert do you mean?"

"Well, for example."

"I can't think that far ahead. It's taken me about a month to get him to commit himself to next weekend. Besides, he's done it before, marriage, says it's no good."

Around them in the bar the men's voices boomed and subsided, allowing them safe intimacy inside the roar of strangers. Occasionally explosions of greeting or laughter would rock the room and the two women would wait.

"But what do you think?" Nellie asked.

"In cases like that," Rebecca smiled, "I let him think for both of us."

"But Rebecca," Nellie insisted; she felt she had her sister pinned inside the noise. "You used not to let other people make decisions for you. You remember how head-strong you used to be, and impossible?"

Rebecca sat a little straighter on her stool. "Exactly," she said, "impossible. Life doesn't work like that. Look, there's a table, let's move."

"But how did you *see* it before?" Nellie continued when they were seated again, "Didn't you see your life differently before, when we were all at home, you and me and Sara and Louisa?"

"God, Nellie," said Rebecca, "didn't you?" At the adjacent table three gentlemen returned to their earlier conversation, a little downcast by what had been offered and then taken away so soon. Where Rebecca and Nellie sat, head to head in talk, there was nothing for them.

"If you really want to know, Nellie," Rebecca said, "I used to see myself never leaving home; sometimes I saw myself as the spinster sister feeding Mother with plastic spoons, collecting her checks from Harry and Jack and calling out bingo numbers to her and her friends on Thursday nights."

"Louisa wouldn't be caught dead playing bingo," Nellie said.

"Well, you get the picture. Of course, Nellie, I wanted to get married before all this. The men haven't been there, that's all." She leaned forward, hoping none of this would carry.

"But why haven't they?" Nellie asked in a perfectly loud voice. "Why were the men always there in Louisa's generation and not in ours?"

"Well, do you think that's true?" The man opposite was beginning to smile. "And why are you speaking like this? There's Hugo."

40

"He's English."

"Jack was English. Nellie, this is silly. Mother's life was because of Mother. Ours are ours. There hasn't been a war. I mean there has, but the men haven't all been wiped out." She looked across sternly at her audience. "They're around, they're just not very thick on the ground. At my age they're mostly married anyway."

"Or divorced and coming round for more."

"No, like Robert, not coming round for more." Rebecca was silent for a while, waiting for the noise of the next door table to cover her remarks. "Or they're boring, or"—she looked around her in the bar—"bad in bed, you wouldn't believe the range of the badness, or else crazy— don't laugh, Nellie, I mean dangerous, or gay, of course, or . . ."

"Or just gone," said Nellie. "Just gone away."

"He's coming back," said Rebecca.

"I wasn't meaning Hugo only," said Nellie. "Ricky too."

"Oh yes," said Rebecca, "very altruistic." She leaned back and looked at her sister. "What have you got up your sleeve, may I ask, while the cat's away? And away, I may say, for about a week. Before you bemoan the dearth of men, you have to hang in a little longer . . . Actually, Nellie, what *are* you up to? You're rather dressed up tonight. Who is this old friend?"

Rebecca, together with the three neighboring men, looked at Nellie.

"No one," said Nellie. "I told you, an old friend."

"Ha," said Rebecca, now positively playing to her audience, and wiggling happily the shoe on the other foot.

41

"Old, eh? Male or female, Nellie, straight or gay? Sane or crazy?"

"Richard Connaly," Nellie said morosely. "Male, straight, or used to be, and doggedly sane."

"Sounds like a rather dull evening," said Rebecca, "for which you have dressed, it seems to me, rather stunningly. What would Hugo think?"

"Hugo knows."

"Goodness."

"Connaly is a very old boyfriend, Rebecca, you may even remember him. Anyway, I couldn't say, 'No, my husband will be away and I must stay home.'"

"Of course not," said Rebecca. She was in good spirits now, partly because the next door table looked like it was about to ask for its check and go. The waiter, bringing the men their bill, bowed his enquiries to Rebecca and her sister.

"I'll have one too," said Nellie. "Two whiskey sours."

"Good evening, girls," said the largest of the leaving males as he slid between the tables on his way out.

Rebecca looked away, ladylike.

"Actually, Nellie, you know I've never asked," Rebecca said, "and do say if you'd rather I didn't now, but since you're always prodding around in my little moral pond, perhaps you'd allow a tiny rippling of your surface. I mean you've been married five years, you must have had affairs?"

There was a sudden lull in the noise of the room, or so it seemed to Nellie. She waited for a moment before answering, like a tennis server in a high wind.

"Actually, I haven't," Nellie said, and then as Rebecca continued to stare at her, "or not so's you'd notice. Nothing that ever mattered. But that's the problem."

42

"But all things being equal, you'd like to?"

Nellie waited while the drinks were set in front of them on little paper napkins. "Ladies," said the waiter.

"We're going to be dead drunk," said Rebecca. "Maybe it's my sister-in-lawly duty to keep you sober."

"I doubt Hugo would have left you in charge of that," said Nellie. "Anyway, Rebecca, things aren't equal, that's the point, and no affairs can ever be very interesting, precisely because I am married. It's too serious being married. It takes the pleasure out of sex."

Rebecca smiled.

"No I don't mean that, though there's that too, since there's no bad sex to compete with bad married sex when you want to kill the other person and have to make love instead."

"You never get close enough to want to kill the other person in unmarried sex," said Rebecca.

"Who are you looking at?" asked Nellie.

"No one. Anyway, Nellie, I hope the marital sex isn't always *that* serious."

"You know what I mean, Rebecca. Do stop flirting. I mean if it's OK or not OK it matters, it's not the case that you simply cross out a name in an address book."

"It isn't exactly done like that," said Rebecca. "And I am not flirting, just being polite. You always make it sound so earnest, Nellic, like life on a kibbutz or something. Sex with Hugo can't be that jut-jawed."

"No, of course not, Rebecca. It can be very good and very bad and very good. Otherwise Hugo and I wouldn't stay together—I mean, inertia there may be, but not downright masochism. However, there have been moments, I confess, when one thinks the whole thing is never going to revive and then one has had—I have had these things, affairs, flings whatever, but they always existed in relation to my life with Hugo, and that did rather spoil them."

"I can imagine," said Rebecca, but she was listening. Nellie had had this married experience after all. "But Nellie, what did you expect?"

"Well, I suppose I was wanting there to be one that would completely cast me and Hugo out, like ghosts, so that I could go on with someone else. Really in order to be someone else myself. It's very limiting living with one person. You become in a way what they need you to be, what they've chiseled you down to or built you up to, you know, Pygmalion, and you end up suspecting that there are a great number of other ways possible for you. But, Rebecca, you must have a sense of freedom, you can change all the time, you have new men all the time."

"Never stop, do I?" said Rebecca.

"You know what I mean. You can be yourself."

"You think so?" Rebecca pulled her attention from Nellie and tried to summon the waiter, first simply and then as she noticed the man across the way watching, more demurely. When the waiter arrived, she transferred her smile to him, unable to send it flying, indecorously across the room.

"I won't have one," said Nellie. "I'll watch you."

"Suit yourself," said Rebecca. She ordered her drink and lit another cigarette, regarding her sister briefly while she smoked. "Actually, Nellie," she said, "this is only a grass is greener number because that is exactly the problem with single life, its chameleon nature, the anxiety to please, to change character all the time to suit the men

44

you're with. Perhaps it's not consciously done but you end up, you know, in bits, pally with x, maternal with y, earnest with z. You get seasick. I can imagine it would be a relief to be just one thing to one person, even if it did shut down sides of you. If you're bored you could try out other roles on Hugo—you know, as they advise suburban housewives—maybe he'd like it: Nellie the vampire, Nellie the invalid, Nellie the . . ."

"All right, Rebecca." Nellie lit a cigarette and waited for Rebecca's attention. "It isn't that you repress anything. It's just that I am all things Hugo creates the space for me to be. And I don't always want to get my space from him. I want sometimes to be altogether new."

"But if someone else came along," said Rebecca, "you'd just get a different space from him. It's a silly daydream, Nellie, so undignified and so egocentric. You really want someone else because of what they do to and for you. Perhaps we all do. How appalling." Rebecca drank the last of her drink. "So ignoble; perhaps we should do without."

"No," said Nellie seriously, "because then you're just left with your horrible self, watching it and checking up on it and taking its temperature. Living with someone at least is a relief from that."

"How depressing," said Rebecca, depressed.

"Yes," Nellie said. For a while they didn't speak. Nellie finished her cigarette and Rebecca ate the fruit at the bottom of her glass. She had stopped looking at the man across the room.

"You can't fool me, Nellie," Rebecca said finally. "I've an idea there's more to it than that. Rumor has it it can be quite terrific. In any case, I shall pursue the Grail, with

45

Robert or whomever. You haven't done badly. I don't know about these chiselers and welders, but Hugo's pretty nice. You are very lucky."

"Oh, I know," said Nellie. "Hugo is very nice, more than nice, and marriage is very nice and love is very nice. I never said no, and here I sit a very happily married lady, I never said otherwise. Let's get the check."

Inside the cab the two sisters sat looking out their separate windows, as though, deprived of the great noise of the bar, speech was no longer a possibility between them.

"Where are you meeting him?" Rebecca asked.

"West 45th, but drop me on Fifth. I can walk, it isn't really raining."

"OK." Rebecca gave the driver new instructions. "Anyway," she said, "Sara's here for a while, is she?"

"It looks like it."

"Do you think she'll take up modeling again?"

"She's too old, isn't she?"

"Christ, that's a depressing idea. Did you remember Mother's birthday, by the way?"

"Yes and no." Rebecca looked at Nellie. "I remembered but I did nothing. I'll get something next week. She won't mind."

"I think she does," said Rebecca.

The cab pulled to a stop on Nellie's corner. "Have a good time," Rebecca said as Nellie got out of the cab. There was no innuendo, but something in Rebecca's sudden sobriety put Nellie on the defensive. "You'll have a better time than I, don't worry," she said.

Rebecca smiled happily at Nellie. She had no doubt that that was true.

. . . .

If she had chosen to, of course, Nellie could have seen swarms of adulterous possibilities around her. They had been in the bar with her and Rebecca, they now came singly and in clumps down the street. Of course she had to forget the existence of Hugo—that was the point—potential loves must not be dogged by the images of absent husbands, for who can compete with the force of such painstakingly constructed figures, bewinged and haloed by the necessary and wilful blindness of wives, even wives who pride themselves on seeing things whole, like mothers who count on great futures for children they can, nevertheless, acknowledge as present dribblers or cheats. So Nellie, while consciously relieved to have Hugo away, knew it was pointless thinking about other men while he and she were married. There was no conventionality in this, it was simply that things seemed to work to the new man's disadvantage, not because Hugo's hands, say, or jokes, or suits, or love-making were better, but simply because they were more known, and hence more "lifelike." Everything else would be paper-thin and pathetically dependent on Nellie's imagination. Or so she imagined. There would be no harm, knowing this, in seeing other people while Hugo was away, since Hugo was never really far enough away in any way that mattered.

Slowly Nellie walked the long blocks to her meeting place with Connaly, watching the couples and singles approach and pass, averting her eyes when necessary, on the daring occasion returning a smile. Enhancing the pleasure of being well-dressed and alone was the pleasure of movement, the glory of conquest owing to the glory of transit.

The nice thing about being married and husbandless was that you could wander around among the sexes pro-

47

tected from all sorts of assaults and innuendos. Hugo, when he left, became Nellie's invisible cloak that let her play among the gamesmen, risking nothing more than a curiosity about other people's freedom. It was with this sense of inviolability that she had accepted an invitation for dinner with a single man, had even postponed the date of the meeting till after Hugo's departure, the better to enjoy her freedom inside the—in this case—double protection: her marriage to Hugo and the fact that she had already been that way with the man in question, and was thus sort of immunized.

So it was that on the eighth night of Hugo's absence Nellie went to have dinner with her first lover, not the boy she had first loved, but the boy she had first slept with: Richard Connaly, called by her, in bed and out, by his last name only, rather English-formally it had then seemed, or perhaps disdainfully, for the whole thing had been a terrible mismatching and a failure. Yet now she was curious to see him, to get an inkling of what had once been real.

There was no sign of him in the main room of the restaurant when she arrived, nor at the bar, not unless he'd drastically changed, and that she couldn't believe since his voice on the phone had been the same, formal now, more adult, but as they were finally arranging the date, just slightly insinuating, faintly triumphant. In that slight edge of possession, she heard him as he had been, knew that something had continued and that she would recognize him there. She checked his name in the red leather book at the desk, left her coat and followed a waiter to a corner table. There she sat for a few moments in frozen readiness, then slumped slightly into the banquette, took out her cigarettes and ordered a drink, something ladylike but not pretentious, white wine, not Kir, and then recognizing a doomed evening in such self-consciousness, lit her cigarette and had the Kir.

The restaurant was large and busy. Here and there, justifying the Brasserie name of the place, were touches of Paris—in the unsprung banquettes, the milky glass partitions, the brass railings and starched and shining napkins. It was a cut above the average New York bistro—no Métro signs, no Piaf, no gingham. It was just a hint of the kind of place you might find in Paris, insufficient to make food and atmosphere suffer by comparison, but (provided you did not search for the loafers, say, worn by the waiters under their dark trousers and long white aprons) enough to stir the memory. And this was appropriate, for it had been in Paris that the promised-to-be-momentous "first time" had occurred. Nellie wondered, as she held her drink and stood ready to trip back into the bright, expectant air she'd arrived with, whether Connaly had chosen the restaurant out of sentiment for that past, but it would hardly, Nellie thought, have been to his advantage to have done so. Still, the Paris part had been fine, the city had been chosen correctly.

Actually, in externals, the whole courtship had been pleasing to her sense of glamor. She had met Connaly on the first night of a crossing of the *Queen Elizabeth* en route to England, where Louisa's sudden summer marriage to Jack had bound them—hauled like so much baggage out of their American lives into Louisa's "European phase." Sharing that September passage were Fulbright scholars, Rhodes scholars, and exchange students, rich healthy kids

49

from America, sent to act as little ambassadors to the as-yet-unknown exotica of the English public schools.

Rebecca, who'd accompanied Nellie and Sara, and who'd looked forward to this trip as a positive guarantee of romantic adventure, spent most of her time lying sea-sick on her bunk or chasing Sara from the first-class cab-ins, thus leaving Nellie free to take part in the all-night dancing and drinking and the inter-cabin frolics which yet never quite compromised the genteel setting of the boat nor the laudable aims of the transportation. But the boys who had been celebrities in their own schools were now, after graduation, bent on reliving their legends, fueling themselves with tales of pranks and heroism, boasting of girls at home—either true or easy—for the most part, and in something of a panic, "taken," on their last, expensive summer vacations, just before the Englishing that was meant to precede destinies at Harvard or Yale.

Had she not been so surrounded, irony would have pro-tected Nellie, then seventeen, accomplished in the New York style, the mix of bohemia and disdainful good breed-ing. As it was, she was quickly overwhelmed by the noisy troopship of the American ruling class.

She had seen Connaly the first afternoon of the crossing, sitting on a bar stool in the tourist lounge, almost a par-ody of Connecticut in his clothes, the mix (later it would be perfectly normal) of the uniform—sneakers with gray flannel trousers, tweed jacket over red Lacoste tee-shirt. His ankles, sockless, were tanned; his wrists and hands were large and red and stuck out of the tweed like those of a tramp in the cold. He had fine bones, a large head, thick dark hair, good teeth, but a pink, anger-mottled skin that made his good looks precarious. That first time Nellie had seen him he was talking to a woman in her thirties. Between them at the bar were, at five in the afternoon, a row of sticky cocktail glasses, five or six crème de menthes.

And now he was saying, "Nellie," standing above her at the table. And there she was, caught unaware and simply looking up at him, forgetting to smile or to greet him. And then, a little slow, she was up and putting out her hand, smiling broadly as if to say, "Well, what a joke and what fun after all these years," and not, as she was just beginning to feel it, "Perhaps this was a little stupid, perhaps I should not have come."

For a few minutes neither said that the other was looking wonderful. Instead they fussed a bit with the drink orders, and Nellie tried to make a joke of his lateness and of her starting to drink without him. "It's very good to see you," he said finally, and she had inanely replied, "Yes, it is." She was embarrassed by his scrutiny. He was looking at the way she'd changed, and she was unable to sit still while he did so, courteously, and with, really, a very friendly smile. People were meant to change. She had done correctly. Yet when he said, "You look different," she had sensed a criticism and had not said, as she might have, coy, flirtatious, "In what way?" She did not want to hear in what way, at least not from him.

He, on the other hand, could have no doubt that the intervening years had improved him. He was quite confidently handsome now, well-dressed, sleek, content, as though the passage of countless females had gone into the making of this well-being. Even the waiter saw it and stood patiently, humbly, dog-attentive as Connaly said, First we'll have this, then we'll have that, ordering quietly

51

and without flourish as Nellie tried to summon him as he had been that first term at his English school, a month after the crossing. But with the image of the boy Connaly came her own, too, on a Sunday visit, after the bare legs and sandals, the slim linen dress of the ship, herself school-uniformed in egg-colored shirt, green gabardine skirt, green jacket, green tie, the dumpy correction officer that had greeted Connaly, huge and pink in gray flannel shorts and nursery shoes, patient and dignified as he waited for her to suppress the desire to laugh. Then both of them, tormented by the other's clothes, yet charitable, had walked around the school courtyard, green and pink and tall among the dank and scuttling English school-boys. Nellie remembered how Connaly had stopped one of them, book-burdened, sullen, and how his American voice had gone loudly over the wet slates. "Hey, there," he had said, "is there somewhere a guy can take his sweetheart?" At first the boy had said nothing, but had stood gazing in terror, and Connaly had said it again, more slowly, hold-ing firmly to Nellie's hand as she tried to pull away. "Well, no," the boy had said, high-pitched, not daring to imagine what Connaly had had in mind, "I don't think there is." That would circulate, that word "sweetheart," as from a World War II movie, and their look of hicks, or Connaly's look, because already he'd been celebrated and cast out, the Yank, eating with his fingers, sleeping in his underpants.

So they'd spent that long afternoon before Nellie's train and Connaly's Evensong, walking around and around the wet streets of the town, the large red boy and the visiting prefect, holding hands, having tea and cigarettes in the damp cafés and trying hard to recognize in the other the person each had wanted to see that day.

And now here was the new man, grown from that first boy that no school uniform could humiliate, happy with himself then and with himself now, smiling at Nellie as she flailed, willing her forward like a coach.

"So it's really good to see you," Connaly said.

Nellie smiled.

Why was Nellie so nervous with him? And why couldn't she hide it? She smoked cigarettes to calm herself, but they only gave her away, the fact that she smoked so many and the fact that her hand shook as she waited for his light. If this nonsense went on, by the time the food arrived she would not be able to swallow, not be able to cut the beef without scattering the peas, not drink the wine without knocking the water glass. She was not seventeen anymore! And even at seventeen she had been better than that, oh much. Connaly, who, at first seemed to share her nervousness, or at least to accept it as appropriate, was now, she could see, growing warm under the display of sensibility, watching it more closely, and beginning to recognize, after all these years, the homage inside.

Nellie tried to get her bearings by looking around her in the restaurant. In place of those sharp, self-unburying memories of that little time with Connaly, she forced on herself the sights of the dining-room—the glints of silver and glass, the movement of well-made-up faces—and the sounds of waiters and customers, serving and swallowing, eating and talking, like the noise of a well-tended machine. But, inside this tableau—if the parts were bared—less comfort.

For example, on Nellie's left, a plump and gleaming

man of fifty slumped on his banquette and picked sullenly at his food. His companion was hard at work amusing him, pumping his narrative by movements of hands and head, glittering, tripping, desperate to please and happy to seduce, yet dancing on coals for the sake of some contract made, this flash of the good life, the promise, perhaps, of times to come. And yet it seemed to Nellie, too, that the younger man plied his charms until they spilled over in squeals, out of the private space, on to the awareness of other diners, and that these miscalculations of volume and gesture had a purpose beyond the present squirm of the older man, to force the recognition, perhaps, that here was the elder dressed up like a sow's ear to please this tinsel boy, that though tonight he would pay the bill and decide the terms, other nights there would be when he would gladly exchange for his solitude a much wilder display and mockery of his needs.

And, over Connaly's shoulder, among the young couples, some too careless and beautiful even for sex, still fascinated by the simple display of power, the silken leg or sudden, grace-confident movement, there were those couples doggedly paired, out of place in this restaurant, and presently paying for the ambition that had brought them. In a corner, where the maître d' had placed them, sat an unhappy gray-fleshed man with his over-dressed wife, both of them feeling less lovely than they'd imagined possible, and not having the good time they'd paid for. On leaving, they would say the food was not as good as they'd been led to expect, nor the place as amusing. Overrated they'd say, and abysmally expensive.

Among such unhappy diners, it seemed to Nellie, the waiters hovered and bobbed, gliding through the tables like protected swimmers through scenes of underwater carnage. And like a slapstick comedian walking into glass, Nellie felt herself hit by it, this recognition of what there had been with Connaly, that had fed her present nervousness, the quality life had then, the constant—what? humiliation of it, that first love. And now, protected only by the elegant table that separated them, she had to endure its all coming back to her, sharply, while she forced back the manners of a cornered virgin and connived at the image of the carefree and willing reunion. "And where after Harvard?" she sang.

Horrors of infancy, that was all. Another life long ago. No possible reason to slip into the stances of the past or give ground in a present tug-of-war. There were thirteen years between them. And now, in a flush of desperation that these might begin to disappear, Nellie tried to name the parts of the past, almost incanting them as a charm against her time with Connaly: school and graduate school, her return to Paris (unfortunate, but true—only the barest flicker of Connaly's lids as she named the city), the marriage to Hugo.

"English, is he?" Connaly said.

Nellie thought she detected a little of Connaly's chauvinism in the question, but she couldn't be sure. "Yes," she said, "English."

"And then you both came back here. He's a writer, right?"

"Yes."

"And you do something in art, right?"

"I'm working at the Museum of Modern Art. We're doing an Abstract Expressionist show next year."

Connaly said nothing.

"Jackson Pollock, de Kooning . . ."

"Yeah, I know. So is that nice?"

"Mostly."

"You want some more wine?"

"Thank you."

For the past ten or eleven years Nellie had barely thought of Connaly. The past was dead. *Requiescat!* And yet even this accounting of it was a kind of involuntary giving of gifts, little ignitable, dischargeable gifts. She knew, or could guess by what he offered her, that his marriage had failed, that he'd come to New York to start again. And he knew . . . But what did he know, and how could it ever harm her, Nellie, safe inside her own life with her friends and her job and her family and Hugo, and further protected from something that had happened thirteen years ago by the thirteen years themselves, all those other loves and triumphs and failures and events that this steak-swallowing, teeth-flashing, silk-tied, connection-claiming Connaly had had no part of.

"I've thought about you a lot over the years," Connaly said. He waited for her and smiled.

On the boat on the third night of the crossing, Connaly had sat with Nellie at the chrome-rimmed table that was nailed to the floor and that rocked with the ship as the drinkers at the bar had groaned in time to the waves. "How many lovers have you had?" And though she had been surprised that the intimacy that came from so many hours spent drinking together should bring them only there, she had told him. "But why?" Nellie had asked, flattered, when he refused to believe her. "You just don't

56

act like a virgin," Connaly had said. That was annoying of course, not the possibility that she appeared so, but the realization that she was in the company of so crude a categorizer. Yet Connaly was sure he knew the signs, and her refusals were simply taken to mean that she didn't want *him*.

Once, in a fury, with his hand still down her back— these little advances were nightly gained—he had pulled himself away and shouted that there was something wrong with her, that she didn't enjoy what you were supposed to enjoy, "a goddam backrub, for shit sake." After that, blackmailed by that word "frigidity," she had let him kiss her, and undress her, though he took forever and she got cold, and lie next to her on the narrow bunk. But nothing more, because, as she told him rather gravely, she did not love him. "I don't believe," she had said, and fortunately that line was familiar to him, "in sex without love."

Unable to have her in the present, Connaly had comforted himself with thoughts of the future at the same time as he consumed her past. He was obsessed by the image of her boyfriend in New York. At such moments when he wasn't charming her with tales of drink at Choate or performing card tricks on the rumpled bottom bunk of his cabin, he would beg for details of Patrick, his looks and (Connaly's mother would have been proud) his background, and did Nellie love *him* (gravely again, Nellie would nod, yes. Too sacred for jokes, Connaly), and what they had done together if they hadn't been to bed.

So, like Scheherazade, Nellie had gradually surrendered all kinds of memories to his appetite for them, paying for her temporary freedom with the silly tales, becoming less and less scrupulous (quoting Patrick's love poems, re-

57

telling his jokes), hoping to keep the inevitable sentence away.

Up and down the long ship they had walked, the irritated Connaly holding on to the gesticulating Nellie as she told about nights out in the Village till four a.m., Patrick and the drinking Jesuits, how he was an actor, and "very, very beautiful" ("Naturally," Connaly had said sullenly). What she didn't tell Connaly was that in love though she was, and believing Patrick to be Stephen Dedalus though she had, she had nonetheless played for his Aquinas the Holy Virgin herself, all too successfully, so that she remained, in her cowardice, chastely adored.

And after the nightly contortions of memory, convolutions of theology, Nellie had managed to get to the end of the crossing with her frigidity intact. There, on that last morning as the rain drifted over Southampton harbor, she had left with Sara and the still-retching Rebecca, having promised to Connaly everything she had wanted and been unable to deliver to her Jesuit love. But before such profanation there would be the boys' school and the girls' school and the separation of the sexes. And for that relief Nellie had felt much thanks.

But now, thirteen years later, at thirty, it was silly to be fending Connaly off with tales of the past. All she had to do was smile demurely and say no, that is assuming he was even going to ask her. Whatever was she still so fearful about? Just look how pleasant he was being, and if she were fair, charming. And look how pretty he is. And you know him, no mystery, nothing but this nice evening, which, Nellie, please, just relax and enjoy. Yes.

"So how long is your husband going to be away?"

Nellie looked at Connaly, but he was simply being so-licitous, not the least pouncing.

"I mean it would be very nice for me to see you again, if you've any time." All urbane and stepping back, as if to say, "Of course I understand you do not have affairs but we are old friends after all, surely we can eat together without fuss."

And she, not wishing to appear a Calvinist matron, smiled, delighted at such a prospect, if for no other reason than she might thus get rid of him that much more easily tonight.

"What are you up to over the weekend?" Connaly said.

"Not much."

"How about this Thursday?"

"OK, Thursday."

"And if you still like me after Thursday, how about Saturday?"

"All right," Nellie said, smiling. And in her ears she heard her own cheerful voice as it would sound within the next hour or so: "Thank you so much for a lovely time, and see you Thursday!" And soon after that she heard the happy sound of her front door closing and the bolts going home and the chains slotting in. In exchange for such pleasure, who would not sign away the future?

SARA SLEPT next to the cat and, like him, curled up against the assaults of the day. Slowly the morning light had entered her bedroom, casting its arc wider and stronger each quarter-hour, while she kept her back to it, like an importuned husband feigning sleep. Like the cat she could hear the noises of the house and her own deep breathing and yet sleep on. Detecting the sadness in her own sound, she did not hurry to find the cause; she simply noted the poison and crawled further inside her sleep.

Down the corridor came Louisa rattling a tray. "Sara, darling," she said, "you must wake up. It's not normal to sleep so much, you'll get sick. I've brought you black coffee."

Sara turned around slowly and opened her eyes on to her mother's face. She could see that Louisa was beginning to look more troubled every morning. She took her coffee and tried to smile. "Jet lag," she said feebly.

"Not after one week, my sweet," said her mother. "What do you want us to do? Shouldn't Ricky be out here with you?"

Sara drank the coffee in small hot sips as though in a hurry to get it down, as though late for something. Then, like a small child, handed the empty cup to her mother. "No, please," she said.

"Well, what are we going to do?' Louisa used a conspiratorial voice, as though planning an outing. "What should be done?"

Sara pulled her shoulders and chest out of bed and leaned back against the pillows, heavily, because though she had slept this past night like the previous seven more than ten hours, she was not rested. She looked ill, and, now that her tan had faded, a yellowy pale color that looked worse in Louisa's nightgown. Over her bony shoulders and flat chest, the décolletage was somehow ludicrous, as though worn by a drag artist. Louisa had a sense of her wardrobe being parodied; she made a mental note to buy Sara some pajamas. Where the nightgown gaped as Sara leaned forward Louisa caught a glimpse of her daughter's boyish breasts, practically the same rosy little points Sara had had at thirteen when, worried about her body and the lateness of her adolescence, she had trailed after Louisa and Rebecca, demanding they admit that certain people never got periods or breasts but grew into men instead of women. That had been for a whole year Sara's nightmarish preoccupation, based, as Louisa remembered, on the condemning prominence of Sara's ribs. Eventually, forced by the inundation of literature on hermaphrodites, illustrated by photos of unsmiling children with blacked-out eyes, Louisa herself undressed and lay down in her bra to show her daughter that she too, under the unequivocal breasts, had ribs in swelling cages. And though the promised lovely bosom had never really arrived to show Sara that her mother was right, the period had come, and for some reason, alarming and burdensome as that must have been, Sara had been inordinately happy to have it.

"What do you want us to do?" asked her mother.

61

"Nothing, Mama, please. I just want you to do nothing, and not worry."

"That is not my way," said Sara's mother. "If there's something to be done, I'd like to do it. Do you want to go away somewhere for a while?"

"Where?" asked Sara.

"Anywhere. Bermuda. Bermuda would be nice."

"Alone?"

"You'll get cold," Louisa said, pulling the sheet up under her daughter's chin, more to hide the dismal sight of her orchid nightie than to protect Sara. "I suppose Nellie might be able to get away. Rebecca works too hard."

"Oh, Mama, Nellie would hate it and so would I, and anyway those trips never did any good."

"Didn't they?" asked Louisa. "I thought you'd both always had a lovely time. You always came back glowing."

"Not really," said Sara. "Just tan."

Louisa sighed. "Well, will you get a divorce then?"

"It's such a big fuss."

Louisa had not expected this response. "Yes," she agreed, "but it settles things."

"I'd just have to start from scratch," Sara said.

"What do you mean, darling?" said Louisa, unconsciously stroking her daughter's wrist.

It was the sight of her mother's hand and its proximity to Sara that suspended her then for a few seconds. A strong wave of memory hit her and caught her unprepared. It was not the feel of her mother's hand over hers, but rather some conjunction of shapes that triggered a sense, so long unhoped for, of overwhelming security and happiness. It was so strong and so rooted in the past that Sara could neither feel sorry for herself now nor nostalgic, but merely greatly surprised, rather at the gift of memory than at the thing remembered.

"Mother," said Sara, suddenly looking up at Louisa.

"Sara?" said her mother, unused to this formal name.

"I can't keep doing it."

"What?"

"Starting again, coming back tanned from Bermuda and scrapping with Nellie and starting all over and getting beaten again. I'm too feeble and too tired."

"Nonsense," Louisa started to say, but Sara stopped her.

"I don't want to think about divorce now, and I don't want to leave Ricky, because I'll just have to start all over and I'm sick of it. I just want to be left alone. I can't manage any other way. I haven't really got the strength not to be alone; it's such a fight all the time, you can't breathe, you can't get your breath." Sara's voice came in small chokes. It was the first sign Louisa had had that her daughter might be more than simply exhausted. She put her arm around Sara over the nightgown, an odd sensation, like comforting yourself. At the same time she knew she held baby Sara, for whom she, Louisa, had been always the same, always holding and comforting, all their life together, not Rebecca, not so much Nellie, but always this last baby. "Sara, my darling," she said, herself on the verge of tears, "yes, you must cry, you always cried here, right here," and she adjusted her shoulder so that the sacred place could be reached.

"It's too exhausting living with another person, Mama," Sara said, wiping her mother's shoulder where it was wet. "I just want to stop here, I'm not strong enough. I'm not as strong as you or Nellie or Rebecca or anyone else. You don't know what a fraud I am and a coward."

"My darling, darling child," said Louisa, alarmed, "you can't know what you are saying. I promise you this is nothing, nothing and you will be yourself again soon."

"But this is myself," Sara cried. "This is how I am, scared and tired all the time, you've no idea. I hated being married, I didn't do anything right."

"Nonsense, it's Ricky who's not done things right, and besides there is nothing to do. You are talking nonsense, my baby," she said, rocking Sara in her arms. "My baby, baby, this will seem nothing in a few years, you'll have new men friends and perhaps a new husband and lovely children as I have had and we'll just forget about Ricky if that is what you really want, but he mustn't, that would be too wicked, be allowed to spoil your life, you're just a baby!"

"I'm not, I'm not," said Sara, pushing away from her mother and pulling up the sheer tiny sleeve, where it had fallen Lana Turner fashion down her arm. "I'm older and more tired than you think and I can not do it again."

Louisa having relinquished the madonna grip on her daughter, Sara sat back, tear-stained and wild, like Burne-Jones's Beatrice on her cot.

"Sara," said her mother, "Sara, listen to me. There is no choice in this matter. You must either go back to Ricky and make something of this marriage, with his help of course, or you must get a divorce and begin again. But if you do divorce, you are obliged, morally obliged, to yourself and your sisters and me, but mostly your obligation is to life," Louisa raised her hands a little in to the sunlight, "to begin again. There *is* no stopping except for death. You are twenty-six; to speak of living the rest of your life alone is absolutely immoral. Of course being in love, having lovers, finding them, losing them, being hurt, worse, destroyed, all that, of course it is hard—that is the very definition of it—but you have no choice in this matter, none. Because that is all there is, and all you've been given, all your beauty and intelligence and gentleness is for that. And if you don't find someone you love for a year or five years, well, too bad, you must go on looking, there is absolutely nothing else to be doing in the world. Anything else, everything else, is nothing, absolutely nothing."

Louisa had rather surprised herself with the force and severity of this speech, and as it subsided she began to feel a little embarrassed, as though she'd revealed some unfortunate inclination for which she might ever after expect to be teased. While her mother's outburst raged, Sara had remained backed up in her corner with Louisa's nightgown drooping, looking like a fantasy of rape, but saying nothing. The cat had long ago disappeared in the noise. Now, once again it was deadly quiet in the noon-lit room.

"Why?" There was a flatness to Sara's voice that frightened Louisa. "I haven't got the strength, Mama. It takes too much. And why can't I live alone? People do it all the time. Why do I have to marry just because you marry and Nellie did? Rebecca's single."

"Not by choice, I'm sure. And I think she'd be very unhappy and a little surprised to think she was an example to you in that respect."

"You're single at the moment, you're not dying. You could stay single and survive."

"Well, of course, Sara, don't be silly. I am an old woman," Louisa waited a moment for contradiction, but seeing there was to be none, continued, "and I have had my marriages, as you shall have yours. Singleness for women is only a temporary state. That is the way of the world, and always will be."

Sara said nothing for a while. The sun was now fully on her face, catching her unnaturally white and still, like a stage-lit Pierrot. "I can't," she said. "I've seen wives, I see them at parties and on television, they're always laughing, confident. I can't be like that. Ricky scares me for one thing." She looked at her mother to make sure she was listening. "I am actually afraid of him." Something seemed to dawn on Louisa. She leaned towards her daughter. "Does he hit you?" she asked.

"No, but he shouts," said Sara.

"Oh well." Louisa moved away.

"And he frowns," said Sara, "and he looks disappointed, as though I'd failed him somewhere, but I have no idea where. I don't know how I'm supposed to act with him, certainly not as I am, 'myself,' that's never enough. And when I try to be sort of cheerful and wifely and full of greetings, you know, how they say you're supposed to be with the returning warrior, all that, I am so uncomfortable after a while because it's not me. I just don't recognize myself doing it, so even if it works and it never does, it's not something I can remember or feel like doing again. Do you see?"

"Well, you must keep trying," said Louisa, distressed by the image of Sara bobbing and curtseying in white-face, of pool-side suppers and Labradorian looks, by this and the not quite recognized but sensed analogy between that and her own erotic style. "Look," she said, "it isn't easy living with other people. Ricky is a separate person, after all, just like—anyone—like Linda, was that her

66

name, that you lived with in college? Even Nellie, who has the identical background to you," Louisa was pleased by her argument, it was bordering on the scientific. "Even with Nellie it was hard for you, and vice versa, of course, but you were forced as children and it sort of worked, didn't it?" Louisa smiled at Sara, presenting the same face she'd used twenty years ago to explain difficult things or to chastise "a naughty old chair" if Sara had bumped into that.

"Not exactly," Sara said.

"Well, I don't know," Louisa said suddenly, letting her face resume its contemporary expression. "I don't know how I'm supposed to advise you. I found living with Jack difficult, often, yes, and Harry. But that was different. I mean he *was* being difficult. Alcoholism is all the difficulty a marriage needs. But beyond that I remember feeling I was sort of riding out storms and that things were bound to get better. Of course, they didn't always. No, I'll tell you, I used to give it a kind of leeway. I'd say, well if things don't get better by next week or next month or whatever, I'll . . ."

"What?" Sara asked.

"Well, I'm trying to remember. I think I thought I'd go away for a while or have it out or something, but not leave, I don't think, not seriously. Once with Harry I was sorely tempted. I went off intending to stay a while in Capri with the Marshalls, but I got so bored being without him, even as awful as he was then and God, you remember, no you were too young, he could be awful, that I came back, the proverbial tail between my legs. Harry was so blind drunk at the time I don't think he'd noticed I'd gone. I tell you, Sara, that is a large part of the prob-

67

lem, one's own company is so limited and so dull. I'm sure Rebecca stands it only because she works so hard. Even so, she won't stay single forever, you wait and see." Louisa smiled her "Mother knows" smile once more.

"It may be dull, Mama," said Sara, "but it isn't terrifying. I'm beginning to see that it's all I can handle, or all I want to try. I'm not so demanding, I guess, with myself, unlike Ricky, and I am not a disappointment to myself."

"What, never?" asked Louisa, but Sara did not smile.

"No," Sara said, deadly earnest, "I expect pretty little. Just to be without the pain would be enough, really. Plenty."

"Well," said Louisa, feeling unfairly defeated after so much effort. "At least get up, now, for my sake, won't you?"

When Louisa had gone from the room, Sara got out of bed to stand by the window, placing herself in the sunshine. She hadn't meant to state a plan to her mother, in fact she hardly knew she had one until she'd blurted out that she would not divorce Ricky but would use him instead as a cover for her solitude. People might pity the philandered wife of Ricky Byrnes, but they wouldn't, if she were thus married, hustle her off to another wedding. This way she could avoid all those double dates and dinner parties, invitations whose sole aim was to separate her from her single status. As a single woman she was a provocation, crying out for alteration and finish like raw canvas or unfired clay. But if she could keep Ricky no one would interfere. She could have her husband and her loneliness too, an *embarras de richesses!*

And secretly, the other side of this plan began to appeal to her, the idea of not letting Ricky go. Simply by being alive, she would act as a drag weight on his life and freedom and happiness. Forbidden to be his dove, his bird of Paradise, she would be his albatross. She would have it so that he could not turn his head or laugh or walk without feeling her dead weight against his breast, the feel of the harm he had done her, the liveliness he had taken. Why not weigh him down? Why not give him some of her weight, that even here, in her old childhood room, where she'd been playing long before he'd been alive for her, in front of this sun-filled window, on this May-smelling day, held her captive. Why not give him some of that?

Louisa came back into the room, ostensibly to deliver newly ironed clothes to the foot of Sara's bed, but really in order to see if she had risen. "At least get dressed," said her mother, "and I don't think it's such a good idea for you to stand around in your nightie at two p.m. in front of the window. It looks peculiar, to say the least, even if no one is liable to look up. Still, they might mention it to the doorman or someone, and you really ought to be dressed. This is a very unhealthy routine, Sara."

"Sorry, Mama," said Sara. She sat down again on the bed and waited for Louisa to go so she could undress. Louisa, however, seeing Sara refuse to get out of her nightgown, continued. "It seems to me that Eberhardt is a little too easygoing with his patter about nature taking her course. I wonder if we couldn't do better? Rebecca said something last time about a doctor friend. Perhaps we should let him see you? What do you think, Sara?"

Sara said nothing.

"Well, I think it might be a good idea."

"It doesn't matter," said Sara.

"Well, I think I will tell her. In the meantime, darling,

do try. Have a bath, put some clothes on, smarten up a bit. Look at the weather, Sara, how can you stay in bed on such a day?"

Sara sat on the bed and said nothing.

"All this will pass, darling. I do promise. It is as I say."

Sara looked up, "What is?"

"Love," said Louisa, a little anxiously. Now a little braver, "It is not to be scorned."

"I don't scorn it, Mama," said Sara, smiling brittly, "I just don't choose it."

"Well, there is no choice," said Louisa. "You will see. Life is just too dull and too dismally hard without it."

INSIDE HER OFFICE on the fourth floor of the Museum of Modern Art, around five o'clock on a Monday afternoon, Nellie sat amid framed posters of previous exhibitions, her back to the green plants lined along the windowsill, where the late-May air entered and disturbed them, and her, as she worked. With a blue pencil she marked between paragraphs of the exhibition catalog typescript the places where illustrations were meant to go. From time to time she took a color slide from a series of piled envelopes in front of her, turned on her swivel chair into the window light behind her and studied the back-lit transparency.

The printing of the catalog was going to be a long and expensive job, with a lot of color and a lot of supervision that the color was correct. The text, however, was more or less settled, and any last-minute changes had to be made at this stage, since alterations would cost too much later on. Nellie had wanted a lot of alterations, or at least additions to the text. She'd been arguing about them for weeks. Lately, what with one thing and another, she'd rather given up.

Four years ago, Nellie had not had this job at the Museum and had not been able to decide what she ought to be doing. Hugo didn't care what she did, he'd said, as long as she was happy. Half-heartedly looking for work, Nellie had been happy for months, waiting for the right job. Slowly, she'd become absorbed in the exotic life of the housewife, painting the kitchen, papering drawers, paying daytime visits to friends.

One lunchtime, Hugo, then working on the staff of a magazine, had come uptown to join Nellie at a restaurant, one of the kind built for a female clientele, with little tables serving ladies' food—quiches, salads, Perriers with lime—itself part of a larger store that sold delicacies in glass cases. On the balcony that overlooked the shop, Hugo and Nellie had watched the women coming in to make purchases, as they slowly paraded in front of the cases in twos and threes, elegantly coiffed and dressed, silently choosing, or discussing, calories and costs, freshness and seasoning—slowly, as though they might spend whole days sampling and deliberating on edibles for themselves and their husbands, on things to be taken home and unwrapped, set out on matching plates, offered, tasted, criticized, consumed.

In and out of the snapping bags came wallets and purses with zips and pockets and pouches to put all the secret things that women cannot venture forth without, and as the noise of all that zipping and snapping shut and rattling of purchases came up to where Hugo and Nellie sat depressed on the balcony, Nellie got a vision for the first time of women as men in their blackest moods might see them, distorted and irretrievably harmed by the passage of such days, the anxious satisfaction of needs and organization of pleasures, spending and wrapping, unwrapping and swallowing, day after day until the end. That afternoon Nellie had phoned all the places she knew

there would be possibilities of work, and had fallen grate-
fully on the offer of a job, in one month's time, as re-
searcher in the Department of Painting at the Museum.

At first, Nellie had been overwhelmed, after so long at
home, by the apparently purposeful complexity. There
were so many distractions that it was a fight often to do
what was there to be done, and in that fight one was likely
not to notice how little that might be. The whole system
with the telephones, for example, was incredible. Nellie
would make four calls and everyone would be out, so that
whatever it was that was needed had to wait until the calls
were returned, when Nellie might be out or at a meeting,
coming back to find the message that they had called but
were leaving for the day, the week, the summer vacation.
When she did get through, it wasn't possible simply to
get what information was wanted, instead there was the
"pleasantry" to go through, the big "his" and sincere hel-
los, names right and jokes about the weather or the week.
If there was something wrong with the tone, it was always
detected by the other party and Nellie would have to stay
on the phone until the rapport wandered back and peace
was made. Otherwise, the failure would be remembered
next time, and made to count against her.

And when people came into the room where she was
working, holding with one finger on to a paragraph, at the
top of the page, in the middle of a book, stacked high on a
book-covered desk, and typing with a finger of the other
hand, she would still be expected to do the "his" and
smiles and long, leisurely anecdotes, interspersed with
reassurances that nothing was being interrupted.

And perhaps nothing was, because office life certainly
seemed to be among the least efficient ways of getting

things done, really another form of social life, paid for of course, though only just, but like parties or barracks togetherness, just one form that people have of not being alone, for which purpose wandering around in shops in twos and threes and interrupting shopkeepers seemed to Nellie as good a solution as this.

Of course no one at the Museum was there for the money, nor, if they'd been asked, for the joys and humiliations of ranked social life. They were there to further the good name of art, to broaden its appeal, and make it lovable. Towards this end, Nellie and her colleagues had been working for the past year, removing the fustian from Abstract Expressionism, underplaying the sad histories, highlighting the dynamic brushstrokes and cheerful color. In place of the romantic irrelevancies that kept cropping up in Nellie's paragraphs about the painters, the curators wanted facts, dates, visual description. References to tragedy, struggles, authenticity—never mind that this was the very vocabulary of the artists themselves—were, Nellie was told, really only a waste product of the art itself, which was pure color and shape and historical antecedent, as any art student could tell her.

Nellie really ought to have argued the anti-formalist case a little harder. She knew that the paintings weren't really just about art, that they had biographical reference to lives led, in one stumbling fit of confusion after another, by the artists, but it would be a vulnerable thing to say so in the catalog, and rather too complicated, for present purposes. The main thing, as the curators said, was to get people inside the museum and looking at pictures.

Nellie took a slide from the pile in front of her, turned her chair and held it against the sky. It was a purple

Rothko from the artist's most cheerless religious period. Against the bright May sky it certainly seemed a denial of whatever might in happier mood be deemed to be up there. God, of course, was not going to be mentioned in the Abstract Expressionist catalog. Even Jung had failed to slip in, not even a tiny concession from the formalist faction, at present in full revisionist power at the Museum.

"A Jungless Pollock, a Gaudier-less Gorky, a Godless Rothko." Nellie spoke aloud inside the empty room, her habit ever since she'd graduated to the single office. Actually, her previous companion had simply been fired, thanks to the famous Recession, though secretly, Nellie was sure it was because she'd been seen twice crying over the xerox machine. At the Christmas party Nellie had said to the personnel manager, whose fault he insisted it was not, that if the Museum continued to hire unmarried PhDs on the grounds that they were less likely to go off and get pregnant than married ones (which piece of cynicism the personnel officer had denied) then they had to put up with the effects of a more dramatic private life.

"And why," he had said finally, "do women insist on the right to such public manifestations of their feelings? You don't see men weeping on the job."

"They sit on it," Nellie had said, "and have heart attacks instead."

"Exactly," he had said, "exactly my point. Self-sacrificing, *pro bono publico.*"

"What about wife-beaters?" Nellie had wanted to say, but hadn't. Unfortunately it was rather true about women's incontinence. In youth the menstrual stains, in middle age the menopausal tears, in senility the trickle down the leg. Leaky barges. Even in films women were always being given handkerchiefs.

Some men, on the other hand, Nellie said to herself, as she reached into a pile of Pollock slides, are given paintbrushes.

It had definitely been an era for feelings, feelings delivered on to canvas, and in certain cases uncontainable there. Pollock in private life had been a monster of drink and despair. And Rothko. But they'd wanted it all put on canvas so everyone could see it, all the violence and sadness, so that everyone could see it and yet not themselves despair, because the artist had tamed it all for them.

But not that much, not tamed as much as the art historians tamed it, into the feeble little aesthetic facts, that were to appear, right way up, one hoped, reduced of course, but in full, approximate color, on the pages of Nellie's catalog.

If you'd read it, the typescript in front of her, cover to cover, you wouldn't have the least idea that any of it had cost the artists more than the tubes of paint. But it had cost them. "I belong to a generation," Motherwell had said, "that mainly killed itself in one way or another."

Gorky, for example. It was impossible to understand his art unless you knew the fear that led him to make the work the way it is made: the tiny, intricate drawing with misleading overlying lines, meant to fool; or the disfiguring daubs and stains that later seemed the first, characteristic organic shapes of Abstract Expressionism. And you could not credit the fear, it seemed to Nellie, unless you knew something of Gorky's life: his childhood in Armenia where his family was murdered by the Turks and where he watched his mother die of starvation, where he had to steal and lie to get himself and his sister to America; and then America in the Depression and no money and no recognition until the last years, with their awful brief, headlong train of events: the studio fire that destroyed most of his work, cancer and a colostomy operation, the death of Gorky's father, impotence, his wife's affair with his former friend and rival artist, the car crash that broke his neck and paralyzed his painting arm, and finally, in her own flight from so much pain and anger, his wife's departure with their two children. Anyone would have got the message. On a wall of his barn, Gorky painted "Goodbye, My Loveds" and swung off from the rafters.

But to Nellie the curious thing about Gorky, and what was important in terms of his art, was that Gorky lived all his life as though he knew what was out there waiting for him. Predicting it all, he had called himself a Man of Fate, changed his name to the Russian for "Achilles, the Bitter One," and then, as if hoping to hide from that fate, hid himself in his early years, lied about his past, pretended to be, not the near-genocided Armenian, but a Paris-educated "cousin of the famous writer" Maxim. He painted exact pastiches of Cézannes and Picassos (as if to *be* them, he even painted self-portraits in their style). When he wrote letters to women he copied them from the recently published correspondence of the artist Gaudier-Brzeska, who had died in World War I.

"Now that I have got over the fatigues of the journey," the scrawny, tubercular Henri Gaudier had written to his love Sophie after a trip in 1912 from London to Worcestershire; "Now that I have gotten over the fatigues of the journey," wrote the strapping young Gorky to his lady in Rochester.

77

For years, until recent discovery, art historians had accepted these Gorky letters as his own, pages and pages of another man's life, homely detail, avowals of love and lengthy aesthetic philosophy. But even now that they knew about such plagiarisms and possibly even of the fear that motivated them, none of it was going to affect Gorky studies or what was going to be included in Nellie's exhibition catalog.

"All that seems to mean is that I am an individual—a pik gaudierBrzeska—and that it is my individual feeling which counts the most," Gaudier had once written. And Gorky, approving the sentiment had, with complete disingenuity, substituted for the first man's name his own. Thus the Father of the School of Authenticity.

But in the later work, Gorky stopped painting Picassos, and after teaching a wartime course on camouflage, began, tentatively, to paint Gorkys. Under the stains and strokes meant to make the reading harder (to wrap the confession and thus allow the confession to be made), and not, as Nellie's catalog was saying, to push the aesthetic front further into the all-desirable future, the risk *was* taken and the pain was named. In painting after painting the real thing was there, the autobiographical reference, the explicit, sexual detail in shapes and signs that return and declare themselves, underneath the Modernist mask, as the characters in Gorky's life: a wife, a father, a child, a sexually tormented self. Such figures, if you allowed the biographical enquiry, emerged from under Gorky's late abstractions and came to surface like old splinters, like hastily buried memories, like old terrors one is suddenly now strong enough to see.

• • • •

The phone rang inside Nellie's office, muffled in the carpeted room.

"Hello, Rebecca, how are you?" Nellie switched her phone to the other ear, turned her chair and held a Pollock slide under the light. It was very important not to get the slides printed the wrong way round. With Rothko, Pollock, etc. it was not always easy to read the slides, easier with de Kooning, but still, mistakes were made and it made everyone feel foolish, like *nouveau riche* collectors who have to have their purchases adjusted by visiting dealers.

"Well, I was deliriously happy this morning after my weekend, cows and tractors and lovely Robert. However, Mother called me at work in a state about Sara again, insisted I go over there today, even though I was late already for work this morning, the mud still on my shoes and so on. But she said Sara was more important than my criminals and I could hardly argue, not that I ever can argue with Mother. Anyway, I saw Sara at lunchtime."

"How do you think she was?" Nellie put the slide back in the pile. On the outside of its envelope she wrote, "too green."

"I thought she seemed pretty depressed really. I offered again to bring Robert. Mother thought it was a good idea and getting more urgent. We're going to try for Thursday. Anyway, how are you doing over there?"

"Pretty depressed."

"Oh God, what's the matter with everyone?"

"I don't know, Rebecca, *my* little band of Depression artists, I suppose. All those suicides, you know, Gorky, Pollock, Rothko . . ."

"I thought Pollock was drunken driving."

79

"Same thing, isn't it?"

"Not quite. Not for legal purposes—Alex was very funny this morning. Pissed off that I'm finally coming in late after weekends, etc. He's met Robert before. Anyway, he said Robert and I were ideologically incompatible."

"Why?"

"Alex says lawyers and shrinks have totally opposing views of truth and its expression, that shrinks take everything their clients say as covers for other things, you know, dreams, symbols, slips of the tongue. Whereas lawyers, he says, have to take their clients' word as gospel, declared on oath to be exactly what they think and mean. He means our clients of course, the other side has the liars. Still, it makes you wonder about Robert."

"You think," said Nellie, "he sort of listens to you for an *under*-conversation or something?"

"It's a creepy thought, isn't it?"

"Actually, Rebecca, he's probably had enough of that by the time he comes to see you, probably goes on hold."

"But what if it's a habit of mind? Come to dinner tomorrow with us, tell me what you think."

"Can't, I'm afraid, but thanks."

"What, not old Connaly again?"

"No," Nellie lied, "work."

"Well, call when you're bored of your widowhood. Listen, if you get really depressed let's go to a movie, something really depressing, from Czechoslovakia or somewhere, that'll cheer us. It's not good for you to be alone."

"No."

"So call me."

"Yes, I will. Thanks, Rebecca."

Nellie put down the phone and pushed the typescript

80

catalog away from her, next to the pile of slides. Rebecca's call had really finished her off for the afternoon, with the mention of Connaly, images of whom had been surfacing in and out of her thoughts at work for the past week. She'd seen Connaly twice in the days since their first dinner, once to watch a play, once Saturday afternoon, for a walk to the galleries downtown. Both occasions had been as "pleasant" and courtly as the first. She had lost her first nerves and discovered what those nerves had been there to protect her from: a series of short, remembered visions of those two when young, and the power that had acted between them. In particular, she remembered scenes from their last summer together, and rather like the autobiographical figures in Gorky's late work, its shapes and images came more and more now to the surface of her thoughts.

It was when they were both eighteen, after their year in England. Nellie had gone to spend with Connaly and his family some summer weeks, to see him for the first time at home. The place was a large open house by the water on an island off the New England coast, so exclusive that Jews, even Madras-covered, were not allowed. The Connalys were a large family, the mother tall and bony, with an annihilating voice and yellow linen shorts. The father was pink and pleasant, rather withdrawn. Between the meals, long and arduous, the younger children ran about the house slapping the wood floors with sneakered feet, fighting over games, shouting about equipment, rousing the mother, roughhousing the dog. From that family likeness in the house, of giants and noisemakers, Nellie felt excluded. In the daytime she kept out of the way of the mother and her kitchen, out of the way of the drinking dad, inside her wickered bedroom where she read old *New Yorkers* and prayed her absence wasn't noted. After dinner in the evenings, it was expected that she and Connaly would go out in the family car with the rest of the island young. And this they did, every dreary night, with a six-pack of beer for Connaly, and cigarettes for them both, driving up through the pine and sand roads beside the town dump to make love, as Connaly piously said it and brutally did it in the dusty back of the station wagon, littered with green stamps from Mom's shopping for that gargantuan tribe. There Connaly pumped and panted while Nellie listened to the radio and wondered that all she felt was humiliation, not even repulsion, not even boredom, just a numb and easy degradation.

Once, Connaly had taken Nellie by boat to an island in the middle of the bay. As he rowed into the sun, unable to see her, she had watched him, his brown face sweating and the muscles on his cheekbones rising in concentration. It was then, sitting on her plank of wood, two feet from his, as the oars went in and out, in and out of the water under the hot sun that she had seen how beautiful he was and how alien. He was such an *other* being. She would never be like him in any way, never get closer to him, though he rowed towards her forever. It was then, remembered now with the smell of salt and the beer open under the sun, the slight sickness made by the boat, that she felt for the first time a desire like an enormous admiration for him, and simultaneously inside that, a sad surety of the distance there was between them, unbridgeable, everlasting. For-ever, distance protecting the desire, arousing it, and at the same time, making it hopeless, foolish, ever to act upon it.

On the island of course it was expected that they would

drink beer and make love. Among the beer cans and pine needles, on a sandy patch dotted with other people's amorous litter, Nellie refused. She begged for talk, jokes, language—anything but the body to break the distance, because it seemed then to Nellie that the body could only fail. Connaly began to get angry, he had rowed so far, was this a game, some kind of tease? His anger forced her further out of course, and yet there was that hopeless, humiliating dependency. She could not get off the island without him, he refused to take her back.

Slowly, deliberately, as if in rough parody of the real touching that could never be, Connaly began to hit her, first in prodding movements as if to say, "React, goddam it," and then with a slow cunning, like a savage inventing a tool, in a pushing movement, so that Nellie's shoulders were forced to the ground and her face gave the desired concession to Connaly's greater strength. Nothing was said between them. The insistent thuds gradually lessened while Connaly took up that rhythm and was finally on her and then finally came, violently, noisily, while in Nellie something disappeared, just left, whatever life there had been between them.

All that was toward the end, after the first happier times in Paris and England, but in Nellie's mind it had come to seem the characterizing moment of their affair, as though for the first year, Connaly had been merely biding his time, American-polite and self-effacing in Europe, waiting until he got home to trap Nellie among his kin, and to become magically, comfortably himself, brute, redneck, bully. That, among other things, Nellie had forgotten, under the blanketing amnesia of that term "first boyfriend," "first lover." But Connaly's reappearance and

Nellie's curiously nervous reaction uncovered the early feelings, the mix of boredom and revulsion, the sense of waiting for "love" to start. And then Sara's return, too, carved the edges of these things in Nellie's memory and made Connaly's reappearance in Nellie's life something of a challenge. In those early days, in her ignorance, she had merely put up with Connaly, and when it was over, run away. Now, without really knowing it, Nellie began to harbor an interest in Connaly as more and more she saw him, a sense that she might in some manner—but she did not imagine how—take him on, win back her honor and redeem the past. With a dreamer's logic, she thought she might save her former self by a struggle in the present.

So HUGO'S A JOURNALIST, uh. Who does he work for?" Connaly asked. It was the sixteenth night of Hugo's absence. They were sitting in Nellie's apartment, drinking wine. Nellie had put Mozart on in the background, by way of chaperone, and continuity.

"For himself," Nellie said. "He writes books."

"What kind of books?"

"Different things. About Africa at the moment."

"How long's he going to be away?"

"I told you," Nellie said. She'd told him three times.

"Do you miss him?"

"Of course."

"Do you love him?"

"Of course."

"Of course," Connaly said. "What's he like?"

"Very smart. Very handsome. Very nice."

"Of course. So you're all set up here." Connaly looked around him and smiled.

"Tell me about California," Nellie said.

"Very beautiful. Very nice. Very smart. But boring." Connaly gave Nellie a rather obvious look and went on. "I missed the seasons, I missed the work hysteria. It's all private life out there. Yoghurt and yoga and peace of mind. I missed the outside references in New York, you know murder, poverty, heat-strikes." Connaly smiled.

"Sara says you get sick of the sun all the time."

"Who's Sara?"

"You've met her, my younger sister. She's just come back."

"She was a little flaky last time, is that her?"

"Yes," Nellie said.

"And the other one, the big one?"

"Rebecca's great. She's a lawyer." Nellie was too irritated to defend her sisters and besides, Connaly's awfulness promised her freedom and thus made her cheerful.

"Kids?" asked Connaly.

"Not even a husband."

"How come? She was a lot older than you, wasn't she?"

"You don't have to have a husband," Nellie said.

"I suppose you don't. [Pause] But *you* do, don't you?"

"I do," said Nellie.

"Who are these pictures by?" Connaly asked, looking around him.

"Different people."

"So how long have you been here?" he asked.

Nellie noticed herself fractionally disappointed by the change of subject. She had, to be true, been enjoying the approaches and her own rebuffs and she was moved as ever by Connaly's beauty, all those bones, and the hardness of his face.

"It doesn't look like your home," Connaly said.

"Why not?"

"I don't know. I can't recognize much of you here. Have you changed or is it just that you've got some money or what?"

"I have changed," Nellie said. But the remark seemed more provocative than she'd intended, and Nellie got up to search for cigarettes by way of distraction.

"Well, I hope not," Connaly said. "I liked you before."

"Have you seen the cigarettes?" Nellie asked him.

"I liked you before," Connaly went on when Nellie was still, "because you let me sleep with you," and Connaly smiled the slow, corny, cowboy smile that showed his white teeth, even in the dark.

"A long, long time ago," Nellie said, meaning that it had been too long ago for it to matter to them now. But the phrase sounded rather like a complaint. Connaly leaned towards her and lit her cigarette with her matches, having first unwrapped the hand that held them. He did not give her back her hand, but took it on his lap and looked at her.

"Oh Christ," said Nellie to herself, "let's stop this right here. Take the hand back, we don't need this." And as the hand remained where it was, "This is unbelievably stupid, Nellie. Do look at him, gloating like a weasel with a chicken."

At the same time, Nellie had to admit that it was rather exciting. Stupid and rather exciting, as when she was sixteen with Patrick and there had been all that palaver about whether or not you would be kissed. And here she was fourteen years later getting excited because someone of the opposite sex was holding her hand and stroking the soft inside. So much for the sexual revolution.

Nellie pulled her hand back, but rather vampishly, as though to say she would call the shots, when she chose. But the little display excited Connaly and he took her hand again. "Don't," he said earnestly, "don't pull away."

Nellie glared at him.

And in a second it was over. Connaly grinned in the face of her evident collapse, rather possessively, and moved towards her. Nellie forced herself not to shrink, certainly not to melt. That lovely gulf was disappearing, Connaly's hard, separate face was getting softer, more blurry; then he kissed her and she ceased to see him at all. Instead, she tasted him and his funny taste came back to her suddenly, and with it, a panic that he was, she had forgotten, a real person with his own funny taste, real and thus dangerous, and that she and her resolves were now in some danger.

They grappled for a while on the sofa, Nellie liking it and disliking herself. He was rather winning.

"Tell me about your wife," she said, but she was laughing.

"Where's the bedroom?"

Nellie said nothing. Did he expect her to lead him to the bedroom?

"The bedroom," he said urgently, as though it were the bathroom he asked for, "where?"

"Your wife," she said, and then in shameful capitulation of everything only laughter as Connaly picked her up, the ashtray still on her lap and carried her about the apartment, looking for the bedroom, while she laughed miserably as he made her dizzy turning her around till he found the bed.

And there he put her down and slowly undressed her, making sure that she was aware that he was aware that she was letting him do this, and could have stopped him whenever she chose, but instead was agreeing, demanding that he do this, unbuttoning, moving her shoulder and arm through her dress, pulling her on to her feet, and

pulling the dress over her head. And gently after he undressed her, he put her under the covers and undressed
himself while she watched, no longer laughing, and not
talking and then he turned towards her and looked di-
rectly at her face while he made love to her, gently, touching her as though knowing what she knew about those
earlier times, as though he had come to destroy those
memories. And he succeeded now in moving her, so that
she could summon up no distance for dealing with him,
no irony, but simply gave herself up to him, by way of
forgiveness or capitulation, like a person with no past, or
not that past, and no other present than this.

CONNALY was in Nellie's bed when she woke that Saturday morning. She'd known he was there through her sleep, which had been restless and confined, but still she was rather surprised and irritated to see him sprawled on Hugo's side. Since Hugo's departure, Nellie had begun to luxuriate in the feel of a bed warmed only by her own body. For the past two weeks when she'd woken, she'd been able to stretch her spine against the headboard, move her feet out across the width of the bed. But this morning there was this large, in fact gigantic, other body, hedging her in on her own side and leaving her a good deal less space than she was used to. She looked over to where Connaly slept like a dead weight on her morning. He seemed big and rosy, like a drill sergeant. Last night there had been his beauty and his tenderness, today he was matter, obstruction, an object she'd have to maneuver away.

Gingerly, Nellie slid out of bed, removing Connaly's arm from where it lay across her waist. He did not stir. She crossed to the bathroom, closed the door and tried softly to run a bath, hoping to wash away the night before. She got in her bath as quietly as she could and prayed he wouldn't wake before she was clean.

It was very odd this "otherness"; she must have been in

bed with Connaly in the past a hundred times, more, and she remembered how she'd never got used to him. Last night he'd been "different," but that was also typical. That funny taste never failed to surprise her, nor the grace in his body. She always thought of his body, when she'd thought about it, as so jock, so American, a kind of joke until she was really in bed with it. Then the oaf in Connaly was yielded up like the spirit of a dead man, and what remained was all grace and power. She had forgotten the startling mass of chest and shoulders, the strength of his neck and head, the way his shoulder bent towards her in a kind of courtly gesture, the fine long line from his waist to his knee, and the beautiful forms of his throat, his high cheek and jaw.

Then why now, lying in the soapy water, tenderly remembering all this, was she so appalled by his presence in her bed this pristine morning?

Was it Hugo? Not guilt, surely, not guilt surfacing before the body had even time for gratitude or the sensations of use had faded? No, it wasn't remorse on Nellie's part, not bodily remorse, not at all, but a mental confusion and anxiety about the future. The body rested contented, warm and heavy and wet in the bathtub, but the head—so excluded from the goings-on last night—sucked its sour grapes and whined questions of consequence.

Nellie raised a foot on to the edge of the bath and contemplated her ankle and calf. It was definitely solid, with a sort of life to it; how constantly she overlooked it. She had a kind of apology for it now, a kind of formal recognition, like a government with a foreign power. This morning, unlike other mornings, and without doubt thanks to Connaly, Nellie's body and all its different parts

91

had life and substance. She brought the other foot out of the water and looked at it, and at the way it differed from its fellow. Then she regarded her knees and her thighs— yes, they were very nice, and her very nice shoulder blade, when she turned her head to see it, was very nice, and her breasts of course, the whole party was rather pleasant. Understood that Nellie took no credit for any of this, it was simply Nellie's team to whom she bid for the first time Good Morning. They were her allies, she was not alone, nor was she just one thing, but a whole crowd here, thanks to Connaly and his atomizing powers. And seeing the autonomy of so many parts of her, and feeling how her head had simply usurped dominion over its inarticulate peers, the question now of thought and recrimination and conscience seemed simply more of its petty tyranny. Instead of acting to please her head in this matter of Connaly, but not quite wishing to please her sex either, she would act instead to please her foot or back or thumb, or any other of the outside and disinterested parties.

So she said. But as soon as she heard Connaly stir next door, the rabble chorus silenced, the feet dropped back into the water, and the head took charge once more with its questions and calculations and panics. Christ, it said, here he comes.

Accompanying Nellie's irritation that Connaly was up was Nellie's modesty. She reached for her blue wash cloth and covered her crotch, shielding her breasts as "naturally" as could be managed with her arm. It was important that she appear casual and unselfconscious when he came in. Otherwise Connaly would use her embarrassment if he could, and then her day would never be her own.

"Nellie." The groggy male voice came from the bed.

Unfortunately for Nellie there was no lock on the bathroom door, nor, living with Hugo, had it ever occurred to her to have one. With Hugo she had no selfconsciousness, certainly not this sense of herself as body, sense of her body as parts, like a little foreign language lesson: *voici le nez, voici le bras. Voici la pudeur.* With Hugo she was all thought and sensation held inside the flesh, and that was as her clothes or as her height, simply the way Nellie made herself visible to Hugo. In the mornings if Nellie were in the bath and Hugo was shaving, it was their great pleasure thus to be together—it was their familiarity, that terror of other couples, that they treasured. In separation it was the sight and sound of Hugo shaving as he talked to her that Nellie missed most. Connaly did not belong in Hugo and Nellie's bathroom, transgression here would be worse than his presence in their bed.

"Hi," he said, putting his face around the door and peering, or leering or lurching, or whatever that cat-with-canary action he was making was.

Nellie did not like to have to say "Hi." It was not a word she used. But now she used it. No sooner was he awake than Connaly's will thus triumphed over hers.

He was sort of hovering, not because of the awkwardness of intrusion, but because, evidently, he expected some kind of welcome.

"How did you sleep?" the question seemed rather clinical. Connaly said nothing, remaining above her, just inside the door. Nellie remained too, as she was, her arms still a little weirdly crossed over her breasts, her washcloth just beginning to lift off and float away from what it covered. Imperceptibly, she hoped, she brought her knees a fraction closer together.

Connaly came into the room now and sat on the toilet, riffling his curly hair with one heavy hand, pretending not to notice her awkwardness, or not noticing it, closing his eyes and yawning. Nellie looked at him down the length of the tub to where he sat like a drugged lion. She had not the slightest idea of what to do next, whether to continue washing or to pretend to be just starting or just quickly get out of the water and into the safety of the towel. Too late. Connaly opened his eyes and smiled his slow, corny cowboy smile. "You're cleaning up," he said.

Nellie clenched her knees and did not reply. Connaly looked and then put his hand into the tub and took hold of a foot, the same recently admired for its independence foot, and brought it dripping on to his lap. Nellie remained as she was, though the washcloth was now floating downstream away from its charge. She had to stretch to keep her head from sinking into the water as Connaly brought the foot to his mouth and began slowly to lick her toes and kiss the sole of her foot. Thank God, Nellie thought, there'd been time to wash it first.

Clearly Connaly seemed to want to start it all up again, did not realize that sleep had intervened and that this was not all one scene to be played without breaks. Nellie wanted to cut out what had happened and think about it, or refuse to think about it, forget in fact, just throw it away before she had to put Hugo and Connaly together in her mind. Action without consequence relied on the brevity and disposability of the action. Connaly, however, had no present worries. His arm elbow-deep in the water, he sleepily stroked Nellie's right leg.

"I'll get you some coffee," Nellie said, pulling her leg away from him. She did not like the way Connaly was dominating things, ruining her morning. On the other hand, it was a little difficult to get out, as she was loath to arise wet and pink from the waves, a cross prosaic Venus. Instead, she lay there, having offered him coffee and removed her leg from his paw, but unable to act further unless he allowed her to.

Connaly did not want the coffee. He came kneeling by the side of the tub and put his large head on her chest so that the water just covered his chin in little distorting ripples. Then he forced his arms under her back and tried to lift her out of the bath.

Nellie, struggling, splashing, laughed angrily. "What the hell are you doing?"

"I'm putting you back to bed," Connaly said.

"But I don't want to go." He almost had her out now.

"You'll like it when you get there."

"Don't bully, Connaly, I want to finish my bath!"

"OK, finish," he said, beginning to wait, but looking a little hurt. "I'm not bullying," he said, explaining, "I'm just desiring."

"Good for you."

With that, Connaly grabbed her, watery as she was, and took her towards the bedroom. "I'm not desiring," Nellie shouted, "I'm cold and wet." They were now arguing ten feet between bed and bathroom. There were puddles forming around Nellie's feet, she was beginning to be very cold.

Connaly hung on to her, holding her wet and slippery against him. He tried to bring her legs up from under her but his hands slipped. Nellie tried to pull apart from him; there was a large rude noise like suction.

"Let me go, Connaly," said Nellie as hard as she could.

But Connaly was now fully awake, almost infantile, like a tantruming boy. "Why?" he shouted.

"Because I'm fucking freezing, because I want to go."

"Come to bed," said Connaly, gently now, almost patronizingly, as though placating the unreasonable in *her*.

Nellie felt herself growing furious, yet because she was cold, quite liked Connaly's arms around her. She tore away from him and ran towards the bed, pulling the top sheet out from under the blankets, by now oblivious to her nudity except as the source of her cold. Connaly lunged behind her and grabbed the sheet, as though this were all part of the same playground contest that he was bound to win.

Now he forced her arms down to her sides and held them there. Nellie's teeth were chattering and her nipples were now rigid with cold: these he took to be favourable signs. "Come to bed," he said. Nellie said nothing; bed was where they were.

Connaly pulled his head back and looked at her. She seemed to be crying and angry at the same time. "What's the matter with you?" he asked suddenly.

Nellie said nothing. Then she sat up slowly and arranged the sheet to cover her, and slowly, with dignity, wrapped in the sheet like a caryatid, she rose from the bed.

"I repeat," she said, "would you like some coffee?"

"And I repeat," said Connaly, diving off the bed and tackling her from behind her sheeted knees, "what's wrong with you?"

From the floor, Nellie looked up at Connaly, silently, understanding nothing. But her incomprehension came across to Connaly as adoration, a slave's surrender.

"What about last night?" he asked. He was lying over her, like a coach with a wounded football player.

It wasn't possible, Nellie thought, he wasn't going to ask for a performance rating. I can't bear it, she said to herself, this is a trick, this is Hugo's revenge. I shall never get him out of here, I shall never get away.

Connaly shook her under his chest, as though she were a stuffed toy that made a noise when thumped. Only he was really rather enjoying this. "Last night," he demanded.

"Why are you being so awful?" Nellie asked, pinioned under Connaly's arm and staring into his flushed face.

"And why are you being such a fucking prima donna this morning? Changed your mind since last night? Cowardice or just disappointment?"

Jesus. Male vanity again. She'd forgotten about it with Hugo. He had only his own vanity, not the whole genderload. Disappointment, oh God.

"Connaly," Nellie said very coldly and angrily and hoping to hurt him, "you were wonderful last night, you get the biggest gold star there is. It has changed my life and things will never be the same again. Naturally I'm a little wary this morning, you've knocked me off my pins." She said this slowly and deliberately like a robot, but Connaly said, "Too fucking right. And your superior little number doesn't fool me. You're afraid of me now. You always were. You're scared because I get through." He let her go and stood up, his genitals swinging like turkey wattles over her head. Nellie lay at his feet in her crushed and flattened sheet, an unredeemed Lazarus. She wanted to get up and negotiate the distance to the bathroom. She would have to get him out and herself out with her dignity and her life intact. She lay quietly on the floor thinking how it could be done.

Connaly walked a few steps and then turned towards her, bending slightly to offer his hand and help her rise. The gesture was courtly and long-suffering, having nothing to do with what had just passed. Nellie took his hand like a little girl in a crowd. He pulled her gently and she rose, holding her sheet against her.

"Perhaps," she said to Connaly, dignity restored, "you would like your coffee *now*." A bad move, cheap, triumphing, petty. Female.

"No thanks," said Connaly, "I'll get dressed and go."

Nellie sat on the edge of the bed and smoked a cigarette as Connaly dressed quickly and then left the room. When the outer door slammed shut she felt relief, and guilt that she had not let him win, and confusion that she so hated him and yet rather respected him at the same time. It was annoying that Hugo had left her in the lurch this way, so that she had to deal with men and their strangeness once more. And then she wondered if she hadn't perhaps married Hugo to protect herself from them, and so she wouldn't have to go through these things—long forgotten as they were—the humiliations and terrors of love.

I T SEEMED TO REBECCA as she sat in the restaurant that Robert had been unswervingly charmless throughout lunch, and that maybe bringing him to visit Sara was going to be a mistake. What, she wondered, had been her motive in asking Robert to see her sister? Had she wanted to impress Louisa? Nellie? Not Sara, surely. Or hadn't she really wanted to drag Robert, screaming if need be, into her family with its prosaic little aches and pains, by way of forcing a test of his devotion to her, or so that, by whatever means, he would be there, one of them?

Probably that, but it had been Robert Rebecca wanted in her family, not this Dr Caligari who'd ordered the whole meal as though asking for surgical instruments. She had had to eat her lunch, elaborate though it was, in almost total silence.

"I haven't asked you to perform last rites, you know," Rebecca said. She waited. "Are you going to prescribe those pills?"

"What?" Robert looked up from his plate and tried to focus on Rebecca. In the light of the window, a tiny piece of oiled salad glinted in the corner of his mouth. Even so, Robert looked severe.

"For Sara," said Rebecca, "my sister, of whom we've

been sporadically speaking. Will you give her those pills you've been working with?"

"We'll see," said Robert.

"But you might?" said Rebecca, encouraged by the green on Robert's mouth to go on.

"I might."

"You needn't be so secretive, I haven't any idea what they do, I thought we could talk."

"I don't talk about medicine with laymen," he said and smiled.

"But I'm not a layman," said Rebecca, "I'm family, and besides that, I'm your lunch guest to whom you've said hardly a word."

"I'm sorry, Rebecca, I've been thinking."

This was better. "What about?"

"Something at the hospital, something that happened this morning with one of the patients."

"What?" Rebecca leaned forward.

"I told you, I don't discuss these things." Robert smiled again. "You want dessert or should we be going? I'll get the check."

"No," said Rebecca, grabbing the menu. "I'll have dessert." There was a long wait for the waiter. Robert sat with his back screwed up and his arm slightly raised, like some amateur performance of *Richard III.* He was irritable when the waiter arrived, a nice smooth-cheeked Italian, with whom Rebecca had had already a friendly exchange.

"Signori," said the waiter with a low sweep.

"What's good?" asked Rebecca.

"Would the Signora care to see the dessert cart?" asked the young man, rocking slightly on his black shoes.

100

"No thanks," said Robert, "we're in a hurry. Come on, Rebecca, order something and let's go."

"Thank you," said Rebecca smiling at the Italian, "I'd love to. Robert," she said, all ladylike, "you should have a look at the profiteroles if they have any. They're wonderful."

"Listen, Rebecca," said Robert when the waiter had gone off, "I have not got all day. Do you want me to look in on Sara or not? It's up to you."

"No, Robert," Rebecca said, "it's up to you. You offered your services and that was very kind; you also offered to take me to lunch, equally kind, and lunch is what I'm having. And you have," she could not resist any longer, "a piece of lettuce on your lip."

Robert removed it at once and with dignity. When the waiter returned with the cart, and Rebecca had chosen her dessert, Robert quietly asked for two coffees and the check.

"Have something sweet," said Rebecca offering him some of the trifle on a spoon.

"I don't eat desserts," said Robert.

"And you don't talk to laymen and you don't smile before seven p.m."

"If then," said Robert, "on certain days."

"Why is your life so deadly earnest, Robert?" Rebecca asked.

"It just is sometimes. I'm sorry if I've been inattentive."

Rebecca looked at him. "God this isn't a prom date, I don't want you to 'attend' to me."

"Don't you?"

"I just don't want to feel always so excluded from the

serious side of your life." And Rebecca, feeling she was getting through, added, "I don't want to be," she made herself appallingly cute, "no good-time gal."

"Don't worry," said Robert.

He paid the check. Rebecca never failed to feel slightly abashed by such displays of male prowess and old-fashioned manners. She had not forgotten the first time a man had taken her out, how she had to remind herself that you were not meant to look while they paid, the ritual demanding a seemly blush and a casting away of the eyes, as though what was being pulled out was something other than a wallet. Even now, perhaps, because this was such a formal restaurant, Rebecca's upbringing told her to look away, despite their intimacy, and despite her curiosity. But when they were on the street, she asked him, "Was it bad?"

"All right," was all he said, inscrutable to the last.

How, Rebecca wondered, was she meant to live with him, how was any other than a physical intimacy to take place when there were so many built-in barriers to the relationship: not just their individual keep-out signs, but all that welter of cultural picketing—the intention being, no doubt, the preservation of some individuality, or some mystique, but the upshot being simple unfamiliarity. And if you could not know them, how could you love them? Or were you meant to love simply what you imagined or gradually deduced, until what they were was finally, after arduous speculation, known, after which, of course, one would be crazy to stay?

"Are you afraid of me, Robert?" asked Rebecca as they walked towards Louisa's building.

"Of what?"

"Of me."

"Yes, but what about you? I'm not afraid of your back-hand or your throwing arm or your . . ."

"I'm afraid of you," Rebecca said.

"Are you?" Robert tried to sound surprised; he merely sounded pleased.

"I don't think," Rebecca's tone was entirely serious, "two people who are afraid of each other ought to plan to live together, do you?"

"But I'm not afraid of you," said Robert. "And I doubt very much whether you are afraid of me. Of what are you afraid exactly?"

"Of your being so different," Rebecca said. "Of your self-enclosed life, of your satisfaction with it and with your work. My life seems so open-ended compared with yours; it has more holes in it."

"Well, maybe it shouldn't have," said Robert. "And maybe what you see as the self-containment of my life is something I've achieved with a lot of work."

"Yes, exactly. I do think that and that it's wonderful . . ."

"Don't exaggerate," said Robert.

"But I don't exactly see the place for me in it."

"Every life," said Robert gravely, "has to have a place for someone else. Stop being foolish, Rebecca. I get lonely. I'm not superman."

"You're sure now?" Rebecca sounded depressed.

"What is this?" said Robert. "Why are we having this conversation just now? Is it just possible that you are worried about how I'll regard you after I've seen your sister? You think her situation is going to tell me things about you you don't want known?"

Rebecca was a little breathless at Robert's clarity. "No, I . . ."

"Listen, Rebecca," Robert said gently, "I assure you I have helped friends or their families before this. I am not likely to view you differently, badly, because there's some distress in your family. My non-professional relationship with you will not be altered by your use of me as a doctor."

"That's not what I mean," Rebecca said, "I am not ashamed of Sara, it's . . ."

"You really think I expect perfection, don't you, that any deviation from the ideal is going to send me flying? How then do you think I've survived in the world so far, huh?" said Robert, cheerfully. "How come, do you think, expecting perfection, I have nevertheless managed to remain both sane and [he sort of chuckled] heterosexual? Cheer up, Rebecca," he said, suddenly merry, "my standards are not as high as you fear."

"You're a real comfort, Robert," said Rebecca. "It's the next block."

Under the awning of her mother's building, the doorman with the orange toupee stood waiting for trouble. As he let them pass, he looked anxiously at Robert, but said in the old way to Rebecca, "Good afternoon, meez." "Julio," Rebecca said in reply. The regular elevator man was off and Julio took them up, keeping his eyes fixed firmly on the brass button-panel while Rebecca was aware of herself trying to act calmly behind his back. If she were to show the nerves she was feeling after the conversation with Robert and at the approach of his meeting with her mother and Sara, Julio was bound to ascribe them to some sort of sexual jitter. When they were alone they had an old joke. Actually the age of the joke was the problem with it, for ever since she'd moved in here with Harry and her mother and Nellie and baby Sara, twenty-two years ago, Julio had been asking her when she was going to get married. "Who de lucky guy?" he'd ask, or "You decided yet?" Lately, he'd stopped asking.

Rebecca's mother's door was open when they got to the landing. Gaily, and rather for Julio's sake than for hers, Rebecca shouted into the corridor that they'd arrived. Louisa saw them and gave Robert a long arm, like an actress, "How *very* nice of you to come." And reaching to kiss Rebecca, she said, "Darling, how pretty you look."

They followed Louisa into the living-room, where, Rebecca was pleased to note, Robert stood about awkwardly, rather impressed and unbalanced by Louisa's feminine display, like a provincial suitor of a famous courtesan. Rebecca watched with admiration how her mother's words and gestures both drew out Robert's social good nature, while keeping him firmly in his place, his feet off the sofa, his vocabulary washed. Not that there was any need, of course, but nevertheless it was automatic, this handling by her mother of strange young men. Like an animal trainer, with a little geisha mixed in: half kimono and tea-ceremony, half jackboot and whip. Awe-inspiring, thought Rebecca, and so simple. Robert was now tamely drinking her mother's coffee, by his bearing both enthralled and unsteady.

"Mother," Rebecca interrupted.

"Yes, darling?"

"How is Sara doing? Any better?"

"Well, I'm not sure. I think your nice Mr—excuse me, Dr Savarn—have I pronounced that correctly? I'm so bad

105

with people's names—had better have a look at her and see what he can suggest. I told her you were coming. Shall I get her or will you go in, or perhaps you'd rather finish your coffee?"

"No, no," Robert muttered unimpressively. "Rebecca is right. I'd like to see Sara if I could. Is there a room we can use?"

"Of course," Louisa flounced up, a woman leading her decorator towards the drapes. Robert followed in kind, unprofessionally cheerful all of a sudden, as he trailed down the corridor behind Louisa, basking, it seemed to Rebecca, and overheating quite possibly, in the warmth of her hospitality. Rebecca's own style looked embarrassingly ineffective next to this clean devastation of her mother's charm.

Louisa came back into the room, having deposited Robert with Sara, walking as Rebecca had always seen her walk, with a little bounce, as though there had been in her life underfoot nothing but thick-piled carpets.

"How is Sara, Mother?" Rebecca asked her.

"Well, she is saying quite strange things." Louisa looked uncertainly at her audience. "She says she is too tired to continue a love life."

"Lucky girl," said Rebecca.

"No, she means in her morale. I do think she feels seriously that this was her best shot, that what she had she gave to Ricky, and since that now seems to have been inadequate, doesn't trust her powers to have new relationships. It worries me a great deal, she seems very set. Also, and I hope this will change, she says she is not intending to divorce. She seems to think Ricky's remaining married to her will be useful in keeping other men away."

"Oh dear, not in Hollywood, I wouldn't have thought."

"Well," said Louisa, not humored, "that is what she says. And I doubt she'll be going back to California very soon, she is very down, very down indeed."

"Oh dear," said Rebecca again. "Well, perhaps Robert can help."

"Who is Robert?" asked Louisa.

"A friend, Mother, and head of a psychiatric clinic in Queens. He's meant to be a good doctor, and I know him, which will probably help, although . . ."

"Yes, yes. He seems very nice." Louisa was still distressed by her description of Sara. "He must be very fond of you to take time away from his hospital like this."

"He's not actually on call this afternoon, Mother, but yes, it is nice of him."

Louisa looked down at her hands. All her gaiety had evidently been used up on Robert.

"Have you had any luck with Ricky?" Rebecca asked her.

"Oh, yes," she said, "I finally got through. He's never at his office these days, and I really don't like to hound him at home. I never felt the outraged mother-in-law was my finest role. Anyhow, I did track him down. You know those peculiar machines they have on the phones where you ring someone at home and they pick up miles away? It could have been very embarrassing for me to have telephoned to the mistress on one of those forwarding calls. Still, I don't think it was that. There was male noise in the background."

"You mean chains and weightlifting?"

"Don't be silly, Rebecca, office noises. He was obviously in someone's office."

"What did he say."

"Well, at first he pretended he had no idea how I'd got hold of him, and seemed rather indignant, until I told him I'd dialed his home number and that it was a perfectly respectable hour, unless I'd got all the hours wrong. Then there was a lot of static and noise on the line and then he asked if he could call me back, which he did, immediately, but from the sound of it, from a more private office. Anyway, Sara was asleep and heard none of it."

"What did he say?" asked Rebecca.

"Well he was as charming as ever, I must say. The first thing he said was how nice it was to hear my voice and that he was sorry their personal problems were making my life chaos."

"That was nice."

"Well he is, I have always said so, the most well-mannered boy."

"Greaseball, Nellie calls him."

"She may call it what she likes, good manners are rather rare these days."

"But what did Ricky say was going on?"

"He said, rather touching really, that it was like an illness."

"Oh come on."

"Yes, listen to me. That some terrible illness had affected his perception. He said he'd tried futilely to fight it for months before this had happened. He said it seemed as though he'd just woken up one morning next to Sara and felt as though he were a stranger, or worse, that overnight he found himself changed in his feelings toward her. He said he was unable to touch her, to be in the same room

108

with her without—he was very delicate about it, but it was clear he was speaking of physical revulsion."

"Does Sara know?"

"No, of course not. Ricky said, quite rightly, that that would be the very last explanation you could give someone in a situation like that. It could hardly make things more acceptable. Anyway, Ricky says he fought these feelings for months and thinks Sara had no idea about them, that what she would have felt would have simply been a distance or that Ricky was having problems at work. He says he just waited it out a while, hoping that his old feelings would return as magically as they had departed."

"But that didn't happen."

"No. He says he took up with this other person almost as consolation for loss of Sara. By way of bereavement. Odd, isn't it?"

"Ingenious, I would say. Why didn't he go to a psychiatrist?"

"I didn't ask him," said Louisa. "It isn't something *everyone* does. Anyway, I hardly felt it was up to me *to* ask. He says he still hopes his feelings will return."

"I hope you told him no one's holding their breath."

"Rebecca, it is clearly a painful situation for both of them. He was trying to explain, trying to be helpful. I agreed with him that under the circumstances they had better stay where they are at the moment, Sara here and Ricky there, and play things by ear."

"Well it seems horrible, so unfair on Sara."

"Yes, I know. But Ricky says he didn't ask for this either, and he has a point."

"You mean," asked Rebecca, "that Ricky is really

109

claiming some sort of Kafka business, he woke up one morning to discover he despised his wife?"

"I don't think he knows the literature, dear. He was merely describing his bafflement at not loving Sara any longer. He was trying to be as frank as he could."

"Meanwhile comforting himself with his LA tootsie and expecting us to pick up all the pieces of his change of heart."

"Well what do you want us to do?" asked Louisa in distress. "We can't force him at gunpoint."

"I almost wish we could," said Rebecca. "It's all she wants."

Robert returned looking dour and professional, and setting up sparks of anticipation in the women.

"I have prescribed for Sara some very simple tranquilizers that I hope will let her get the rest that has apparently been evading her in these long sleeps. She should take one at night instead of the sleeping pills she has, one when she wakes and one at lunchtime."

"She usually wakes around lunchtime," said Louisa.

"Well, wake her earlier in that case," said Robert, sounding to Rebecca every inch a doctor, and sounding to her mother, she feared, unnecessarily abrupt. "She shouldn't need to be sleeping more than eight hours a night. Further, I'd like very much, if you were agreeable, to begin to see her regularly, a couple of times a week. It would be best if she could come to the clinic . . ."

"To Queens? Well I . . . of course."

"I could for a short time arrange to see her here. The hours would have to be a little later, of course."

"Of course," Louisa said, "I *could* bring her—Yes, you

could come here? I don't know, I was hoping you could just quickly look at her and perhaps tell us what to do next, perhaps a few pills, but a whole course of treatment . . ."

"Pills alone won't do much good," Robert said, "that isn't what she needs."

"Oh come on, Robert," Rebecca interrupted, "you know the circumstances, she's had a breakup with her husband, it can't be anything serious."

"Are you a doctor?" Robert asked her. He turned to Louisa and spoke gently, "I would like, if possible, to begin to see her a couple of hours a week, we could speak more about what her problems are after that. Or I could find another doctor, if you'd prefer; it needn't of course be me who treats her, but she does need help."

Louisa had dropped her hands to her side.

"But what are you saying, Robert?" asked Rebecca. "Are you saying Sara is actually mentally . . . ?" She didn't know the right word, or didn't want to use it.

"Ill?" said Louisa.

"If that is the way you wish to describe it," said Robert.

"Oh God," said Louisa. "All right, well. Well, Rebecca, there's no arguing. I suppose he'd better come and see her." And to Robert, all geisha spent, "I really could bring her to Queens," she said, "but . . ."

"That is all right," said Robert, "I understand. You are on my way home from work here anyway. We can fix a time and speak about fees later. I'll try to make it as convenient for you as I can."

"That is not the problem," said Sara's mother. "The main thing is to look after the child." She had wanted to

111

say, "for Sara to get well," but she was now fearful of Robert's response.

"Yes, exactly," said Robert. At the moment, it was he who was center stage, Louisa who was audience. "Well, very nice to have met you," he said. "I'll get the office to set something up tomorrow. Rebecca, I should leave you here." Robert bent to kiss her, like a husband dashing for the suburban train. The gesture was automatic, familiar and, to Rebecca, infinitely depressing.

When Robert was gone, Rebecca left her mother and went in to see Sara. She was sitting in a chair by the window, looking as ill people sometimes look, that they have been dressed by others. Sara seemed not to belong to her clothes, not that they did not fit or suit her, but because some act of volition seemed not to have gone into her dressing. She looked tired, and grayer than she had when Rebecca had seen her last, four days earlier, but she roused herself to greet Rebecca. "He was cute," she said feebly.

"Yes, isn't he?" said Rebecca. It was old terrain, but the comfort was gone.

"Is he a new one of yours?" Sara asked.

"Yes, any good to you?"

"Don't know," Sara looked down at her lap. It seemed very far away, and likely to float off if she didn't keep an occasional watch. Her body was behaving strangely lately. Now she remembered that Rebecca had come in and wondered how long the last silence had been.

"I feel so stupid," said Sara.

"Why?"

"I feel I'm causing all this fuss and more than that I feel

so stupid—like I'd been caught out—allowed myself to be caught happy."

"What do you mean?" Rebecca asked gently. Sara was speaking so naturally. She could not be ill.

"I wrote all those letters," Sara said. "I kept telling you to come and get married, come and live in California. You and Nellie must have thought me a fool, or if you didn't then, you must do now. I was just asking for it, being so happy."

"Sara, don't be ridiculous," said Rebecca. "You *were* happy, why shouldn't you say so?"

"Because it couldn't last."

"But why not?" Rebecca was pleading to be told.

"Because being happy is a fluke, like an oddity in nature, or if not that, it's simply dangerous, it's calling attention to yourself, it's sticking out like a sore thumb."

"You think this is some sort of retribution?" Rebecca laughed. "You *are* superstitious."

"Yes. Only as you see, I was right."

"Sara, don't be so melodramatic. You were happy, now you're unhappy, you'll be happy again. It's like a ride."

"You think so?"

"Sure. The only question for you is how long the down part will last."

"But I'm too tired to go up again, and anyway if you're only going to come down once you're up, you might as well stay where you are and get used to it."

"Well, that's logical, all right, but maybe getting used to it is dangerous too."

For a while Sara said nothing. Rebecca looked out the window. When she looked back at Sara it seemed that she hadn't moved at all, not even to breathe.

"I feel," Sara said looking at the floor, "that if I lie low for a while I'll be OK, but that now I am shadowed and unlucky."

"Because of Ricky?"

"I don't know anymore where the feelings come from. I just feel that some solid part of my life is not there anymore, that nothing is sound, or, you know, reliable. I feel suddenly very vulnerable, it's strange."

"It's not at all strange," said Rebecca. "You *do* feel vulnerable if your husband leaves you. You feel alone."

"No, not like that," said Sara, "vulnerable to odd things, like diseases. And I feel suddenly very, very old, like a kind of danger statistic. I feel I'm going to get cancer tomorrow or heart disease or polio, or aging illnesses, do you know?"

"But Sara," said Rebecca, "you're just a child."

"But I feel as though I were aging."

And to Rebecca at that moment, it did seem that that was happening.

"It's a foolish fantasy, I know," Sara said, "but I can't seem to shake this sense that I have nothing to look forward to anymore but bad things, physical decay, other people's deaths, Mama's, yours, Nellie's. I feel I'm losing the world, slipping away, leaving it to stronger, younger people. That's odd, isn't it?"

"Yes, darling," said Rebecca. "And not at all true, of course. God, if you think you're old, how old do you think I must feel? I'm twelve years older than you."

"I'm sure you don't feel twelve years older," said Sara.

"I'm not sure, how old do you feel?"

"I'm very scared, Rebecca," Sara said suddenly.

"Don't be scared, don't be scared, it will be all right. Robert will help, Mama and Nellie and I will help."

"Rebecca, I feel so alone. When I had Ricky I was alone, half the time he was working nights or off with that woman and I was terribly alone, but I didn't feel it. I felt full of other people, full day in and out with my thoughts of Ricky and of you and Mama and Nellie, and the cat, believe it or not. And as soon as Ricky tells me how things really are, it's like a rug that has been whipped out from under me and suddenly I'm on the floor. And not only on the floor, but everyone has gone. I know there are other people around, I hear the noise, I just cannot make out the faces. It's like a darkness," Sara said. "And it's so total."

Rebecca left Sara around four o'clock and returned to work, taking the long way through the park. Alex would be irritated with her for the second time that week, but she needed to think about Robert, to avoid the traffic lights and office phones and be able to worry. It seemed to her that while there was something admirable in the way Robert had taken command over the question of Sara, there had also been something repellent in his professionalism. It was not that she wished him to tread with delicacy over what must have been for him an everyday problem, but rather that she wished him to proceed, in this and in other matters, yes, with a sense of purpose, but with all pores open, all senses awake. For Robert, always, there was problem x susceptible to solution y, where for Rebecca, thinking of Sara, there was only the pain and hoped-for relief, no promises, no guarantees. Robert's methods might get results, but its limitations alarmed her. Like a professional fisherman, interested only in the intended catch, blind to other schools, other swimmers, the sounds and colors of the sea, Robert's mind pierced through to the essential structure of things, scorning surfaces as matter for more poetic, more leisurely natures.

Rebecca thought that she, on the other hand, could take it all in, and therefore could have more. Even now, walking, fixing quite earnestly on this question of Robert, she enjoyed the heat of the day, the dusty smell of the new tree blossoms. You could say Robert was merely doing his job, but that was the point. Rebecca's work life was very unlike Robert's. She was naturally industrious, liked the benefits, the money and the status. With her colleagues she enjoyed a sense of camaraderie, of being all boys together, learning the tricks, identifying the tricksters, growing aged and canny, like a pack of hunting dogs. The work as process she enjoyed. It was simple and fun, rather like a car, Law, a machine to be driven well or ill, happily or in terror, but no great mystery after all, and something that could be done with one's mind and heart engaged elsewhere.

Rebecca's job was also a constant reminder of her arrival in a world of successes and failures, her little tin medal, loved and looked after, but invested with no magical properties. She was not a lawyer in the sense she feared at times that Robert was a psychiatrist. She was instead Rebecca, who practiced Law between nine and seven weekdays, and on some weekends, but whose spirit, whose tenderest heart was to be found elsewhere, in other hours, and on occasion during the same hours, when her mind wandered from her job and her heart creaked behind her desk and longed for something else.

But Robert. Robert really was a psychiatrist, trained for emergencies of the kind Sara represented, little human refusals to go on. Faced with such things, Robert neither shied nor stumbled, but went right down the stony little path in front of him, like a blinkered cob, picking his way through the unhappiness with admirable concentration.

Well, what else did she expect?

But if she were to marry Robert, would she not become not Robert's wife, but simply the doctor's wife? That side of him that had shown itself on the weekend was, she feared, not his otherwise hidden-by-duty self, the genuine blossoming of Robert's Robertness, but simply a subordinate aspect of the same—the shrink relaxing before another long haul in the vineyards of the ill. And if so, Rebecca could expect, not only the frigid lunches and the expert but a touch chilling sex of the weekdays, but on weekends too, her transformation into Robert's erotic recreation ground, his little trailer park, his fishing trip, existing only to return him refreshed and more efficient to the real purpose and arena of his living.

But he was a doctor, after all, it was all in a good cause. And he was her lover, wasn't that enough? Wasn't Rebecca being, not to be indelicate, but in the light of past failures and future shortages, a little too demanding? Well then, yes, she was demanding. And, no, it was not enough, and yes, she wanted more than that.

Only the question remained, of course, was there any more to be had? Was it not a definition of wisdom and maturity to settle for what was available, to squinny at the gift horse, rather than appraise him. Because what else was available—apart from superficially interrupted bouts of

117

aloneness—might be not merely not so good, but quite likely, horrendous.

To be blunt, the beautiful Rebecca was thirty-eight. Not thirty-eight and divorced with children, but thirty-eight and never married. She was perfectly aware that while she had, perhaps, been spared the premature bitterness of the former situation, her own history had exposed her to the dangers of long solitude. Might she not be just a little unaccommodating, just a touch set in her ways? Brittle? Dotty? Well, there was that, and there was the business of babies, since for Rebecca, as for so many others, the baby-producing years had fallen rather prematurely in advance of the marrying ones, and now that she was perhaps ready to start the search for a father, the internal capacity had keeled over, or if not yet, soon would, either that or begin to produce monsters and degenerates, the whole spiteful brood of long-toothed progeny. So they said. Forty, they said, was the absolute limit.

But leaving these considerations, there remained the question of Robert. What chance for happiness in that particular corner? How high should the demands be, at thirty-eight? Higher or lower than at twenty? And then whose marriage isn't a corruption of standards held when single? Of course you would not invent Robert as the dream husband, with the suits and the psychiatrist's patter and the bad tempers. But he was there, should he be taken? Was he enough to jeopardize all Rebecca's stability, put together and propped up for some twenty years, her habits, her freedom, the peace made with herself, her right to be happy, drunk, fat, selfish, all those little rights

118

and pleasures that living with another was bound to erode?

And under all this questioning and not anywhere near the surface of her thinking was a bleakness that Sara's unhappiness had started, a sense that Rebecca might risk all these things and still land in a dismal heap at the other end. So much had her visit to Sara reminded her; for despite her triumphs and her stature as a lawyer, far more than her rights to her habits, Rebecca risked in marriage her very foothold in a world where documents, decisions, actions mattered. Rather than an aberration, Sara's state was beginning to seem the foundation of female life, its rest position, over which all other happy, scheming "normal" life is just an illusion, the fairy bridge over the pit.

Well then, Rebecca, said Rebecca, you either have this present way of living, propelled by a slightly rusting motor of optimism, or else you decide to wink at Robert's faults, Robert's suits, Robert's hours, Robert's conviction that the world is doctorable, and accept him for his company, his intelligence, his skill in bed, always forgetting that—even if you proceed with Mother's faith in the correctness of marriage and some reasonable sense that if Nellie can make something of it, anyone more or less can,— that even so, still you come smack up against Sara. And however much you may wish to think that Sara's situation is due to Sara's peculiar flimsiness, you know that that is precisely the risk, even for tough career girls nearing forty, and you ask yourself is that risk, together with the suits and so on, worth it.

Maybe, said Rebecca to herself, as she approached her office, I should not decide at all, but let what happens happen. Only I know if I do that, nothing will happen except relegation of my shining duty as lady with control —illusion though that may be—over her life. And the fact that Robert may be having this very same conversation with himself (damn likely!), wasting *his* work time, missing tales of transvestitism while he works out whether he can tolerate a woman of my limitations, who insists on giving him sauces made with wine, who prefers an evening with other people to a lot of quiet catching up, hearthside, with the latest psychological research, a little Mantovani in the background (I exaggerate, thank God), should not be considered. I must pretend that this choice is mine, and make it, just as though I were dealing, not with two complex wills, but for solution's sake, with one.

ON A SUNDAY AFTERNOON, a little more than ten days after Robert's first visit to Louisa's apartment, Nellie walked with Sara, perilously among the joggers, around the reservoir of Manhattan. They were dressed alike, in jeans and tee-shirts and sneakers; Sara had a sweater tied around her waist. Despite the clothing, they would not have been taken for runners. Nellie ate an ice cream, Sara was unhealthily pale, and wore sunglasses.

On the lake that glinted in the sun was the upside-down image of the city, like an underwater kingdom. Occasionally, gravel from a runner's heel, or the dive of a duck, rippled the image, so that the buildings scalloped and curled, or vanished entirely into the blue cloud-bearing water.

"That's what we're supposed to drink," said Nellie. "It doesn't seem like enough for all of us. God knows what's inside."

"Dead dogs, do you think," said Sara.

"At the very least."

"I did miss it here," Sara said, "it is pretty."

"From here, and in June."

"Is it June already?" Sara asked.

"Yes."

"Month of marriages."

"Never mind," said Nellie, self-mocking, "upward and onward."

"Where do they all run to?" Sara said as a group of joggers passed. "Or from, they look so haunted, runners, ill and collapsed. They certainly mean business. Shouldn't we be down there?" She pointed to the lower track.

"Down there's for horses. You remember, Sara, Central Park's dangerous."

They walked along at their own pace, mounting the banks occasionally to let groups of runners pass, or walking single file.

"Do you think Rebecca's going to marry Robert?" Sara asked Nellie.

"Has she said something?"

"She's been testing my response sort of oddly. Louisa thinks it's possible. I hope for our sake she does, we might get family rates on my breakdowns."

"Oh, come on, Sara."

Behind them, for whole minutes until he could pass, a small boy with a huge radio trotted. The radio must have weighed forty pounds. It was deafening.

"They carry drugs in those," said Nellie, "they're like handbags. Is he helping, anyway? Robert? I mean, do you like him? How does he compare with the others?"

"All the many others . . . thanks. I suppose you're right. There was Dr Osborne after Gerry; Dr Bernstein for Michael; Sandy Pathek for Charlie, and now Dr Savarn for Ricky. I ought to ask the men to supply their own, like condoms."

"But Robert's OK, isn't he? You feel a little better, don't you?"

"I don't know, Robert's OK; they're all the same anyway, except that one when I was at school, he was a disaster."

"I don't remember that one."

"He gave me terrible pills. I slept all the time and failed my exams. When I went off the pills my studies improved, but by then it was too late. You remember, Mama made a fuss to have me reinstated."

"Oh yes, something," said Nellie, "I was away somewhere, wasn't I?"

"Paris."

"Yes."

"Anyway, I'm supposed to talk about everything until I hear myself so often I get the message, isn't that right?"

"I guess."

"Robert does some talking too, he isn't the woodblock kind."

"What does he say?"

"He says it takes time, of course, they always say that. He says what they all say. You know, encouragingly, just saying how are you and you are fine and you think it's worse than it is, all that. I suppose by the standards of his clinic, I'm not so bad."

"You're not quite *Snake Pit* material, Sara."

"Don't bank on it," said Sara.

"Oh, come on," Nellie said again.

"Before they started running, they never even walked through the park. Not in my time. It's crazy."

"The thing that always seemed to me to be difficult about therapy," Nellie said, "is its complete lack of reference to the outside world."

"What?"

"It's always about oneself."

"Oneself is the patient, Nellie, who else but oneself?"

"You know when you're depressed," Nellie said, "you let things slide, you know, housework, clothes, not getting up, not calling people, not going out, all that?"

"Louisa's been complaining to you."

"No, of course not. But when I get depressed, or actually, just before I'm down, to sort of stave it off, I maniacally houseclean."

"So?"

"Well, maybe that instinct gets blocked by therapy? Maybe instead of talking about the patient all the time, psychiatrists should talk about themselves—you know, wives, dogs, lawns, medical bills, so the patient feels there is someone else out there. For me the housecleaning is a last effort to touch the world, verify objects; people are trickier of course, but if we knew they were there, don't you think we wouldn't be depressed? I don't know, isn't that right? I sometimes feel Rothko wouldn't have killed himself if he'd painted portraits, or apples."

"God, Nellie," said Sara, "are you putting that in your catalog?"

"Of course not. Anyway, no doubt you can kill yourself painting apples."

"I think I'd kill myself if I had to paint apples," Sara said, "or Rothkos. I hate art."

"I don't mean to sound so remote about your being depressed, Sara, it's just that you do seem so fine and the sun's out. The whole matter, under the sun, seems so abstract."

"I know, Nellie," said Sara, "only to me it's not abstract at all, but as real as the reservoir, or your apples, or anything else. Otherwise, I'd love to debate it with you.

124

Unfortunately," Sara said flatly, "I just haven't got your distance."

They had walked by now past the tennis courts on West 93rd, and were slowly approaching the exit for Nellie and Hugo's apartment building, when Sara said, "Can we not go to your place, Nellie? I don't think I could deal with all those signs of wedded bliss. You know. It's a terrible thing to say. Forgive me, but can we go to the museum instead?"

"Of course, Sara, if you want. But there's not much to worry about at home, no slippers by the hearth, no boxes of knitting. Not much more than yoghurt in the fridge; Hugo's been away nearly a month. Anyway, you just said you hated art."

"No, not *that* museum, not your museum, the one we used to go to with Mama, remember, with the bears."

"The Natural History? All right."

Nellie and Sara walked towards the steps of the museum. On the stone landing groups of children stood irritably in the sun waiting for parents to buy tickets or park cars. Among them, on the benches under tributes to Theodore Roosevelt sat teenage couples necking and lighting joints. Towering overhead was Teddy, massively monumented on horseback and flanked by two Indians. By the foot of his horse were two cans of beer and a packet of potato chips. The Indian on the left flank bore the message "BB Boston Out to Bomb."

Nellie and Sara climbed the steps in the sun and made their way among the noise of the crowds in the entrance hall. It felt slightly peculiar to be doing this, like seeing a film at noon. You were supposed to be a child to see the stuffed bears, or a pervert. Nellie and Sara should have been that afternoon bicycling or drinking vodkas in Soho. Instead they walked through the dark, oak-covered central hall where the elephants were. Around them, on the curving back walls of each glass-enclosed display, a panoramic, *trompe l'oeil* scene had been painted as naturalistic background to the animals presented.

"There must have been a staff of twenty or so full-time artists here when it started, don't you think?" Nellie said. "It's a lot of work, all these backdrops. And they must have had a few sculptors for the animal poses, not just taxidermists. Can't you see them, sitting around the canteen or whatever they had, talking about how they got the cranes, say, to look as though they were really drinking."

"Getting the last brontosaurus bone finally in place," Sara said.

"Did they have unveilings, do you suppose? Little red curtains with pulls like the academicians in Europe?"

"Maybe they didn't think of themselves as artists," Sara said.

"They probably did. They probably went to art schools and painted their wives on weekends."

"No, but while they were doing this?"

"No, scientists probably, handmaidens to the natural sciences. Recorders of fact, documenters of the world, I bet there wasn't a conversation about authenticity among them."

"Let's see the shark," Sara said suddenly.

"Do you think it's still there?" Nellie asked.

"Where would it have gone? It used to be down here."

They walked down the long stairs to the room of sea creatures, where years ago, they had walked together, sometimes with Louisa or a babysitter, passing in terror the crusting tortoises and sea mammals, lizards with glassy eyes, suspended in cases the way lizards are suspended in life, just before they dart, leap, slide, horribly quickly.

Nellie and Sara, then little girls, of twelve and eight, or nine and five, would walk slowly, with crawling flesh, forcing themselves to look at the cases, getting up nerve for the most terrifying of all the terrors of the Natural History, the vast green murk where the shark was kept.

Before you got to him, in the dimly lit antechamber where the sensation of underground felt easily like underwater, the cases were so close together that unless you walked with caution you might touch shoulder or back against the glass that held the giant swimming tortoises. Or bouncing from the sting-ray you might lose your balance and be brought abruptly up against him, as he glinted through his sea shadows. You could almost not make him out, though he was there, when finally you saw him, just before fleeing, eyes and mouth of an unimaginable ugliness.

Twenty years ago, Nellie and Sara would sneak up to him, hearts pounding while they waited for their eyes to adjust to the gloom, for the moment of horror and clear seeing. Usually it was Nellie before Sara who would scream, grabbing the younger girl and pulling her out. It was possible that Sara had never even seen the shark, but only heard Nellie's scream and in a kind of misplaced confidence, screamed too, believing in the horror. Perhaps Sara simply felt that if Nellie, unperturbable in most matters at home, the to Sara confusing business of baths and supper and dressing, babysitters and games, if Nellie screamed, then so must Sara, that was only natural.

Now she and Nellie came up to the exhibit, through the neglected cases in the empty basement rooms, looking for the shark. They found him there, still an adept at terror, clearly, but aged a bit, a little wizened around the eyes. Nellie's flesh that had been all too willing to creep in memoriam sat where it was as she looked at him. She searched now in the darkness behind the glass to see how it had been done, how the illusion of deep water and sudden movement had been made.

"He's ugly," said Sara, a little disappointed, "no doubt about it, but wasn't he bigger?"

"I think we were smaller then."

"We really were, weren't we?"

They stood looking for a while as the anticipations of nervousness collapsed around them.

"Why don't we go back to the furry things," said Nellie, "it's a little dull at this level of creation."

Inside the elevator a crowd of children roughhoused and scuffled in baseball jackets and sneakers. "Cut that out, shithead," said one angelic blond to another. "Fuck face," his friend replied. "Oh, do stop pushing," said another, almost quaintly.

"Goodness, what's happened to the garden of childhood?" Sara asked when they got off the elevator.

"Aren't they that way in California?" Nellie was almost boasting. "Do you realize that something like half of these little things have had sex already, or smoked pot, or are alcoholics. It's a little mini-life before high-school. Perhaps they get heart conditions in ninth grade, male menopause in tenth?"

"Then when do they get to be children?" asked Sara. "When did we?"

"I think I'm the only one of us," Sara said, "who ever was, or maybe who never finished."

"Maybe, it's the other way around, maybe your coming home is your way of getting something you didn't get before?"

"Maybe," said Sara. "I did try with Ricky being grown up and married, though, I'm just no good at it. But then I wasn't much good at being a child."

"You were great, Sara," Nellie said, "you were perfect. You were my little friend. I loved having you." She meant it, she knew, when she said it, but Sara didn't know. "Thanks," she said, and sounded far away.

Under large brass lettering of the word PRIMATES sat a group of matrons wearily eyeing their charges as Sara and Nellie came into the hall of monkeys and men. Inside were displays of handsome black and brown apes, long-armed, peculiarly-nosed monkeys, worried chimps that hung from the branches. Above a group of children's heads, smelling of shampoo and oranges, Nellie and Sara read the educational billboard:

(1) Primates have specialized for grasping (becoming upright as they reach and grasp)
(2) Vision has improved, the brain has enlarged
(3) Reproduction has changed

"I like the bit about learning to grasp," said Nellie, "it sounds like Brecht."

Sara continued to read:

Young are helpless at birth.
Maternal care is prolonged.
Young have greater time and ability for learning.

129

"I don't think Louisa's read this," Nellie said.

"That's not fair. She's OK."

"My, Robert's slow," said Nellie. "Shouldn't you be pointing to the mother by now?"

Sara did not answer. "Here's more," she said.

Under the heading MAN, another billboard announced:

DISTRIBUTION: COSMOPOLITAN

Hominids are essentially large, bipedal, tool-using and highly social primates. At present time, judging by its numbers and its effect on other species, *Homo Sapiens* is the most important species of animal on earth.

"That's nice," said Nellie, "most encouraging."

"Well, they wrote it themselves, it may not be true."

Around them in the hall, gibbons and marmosets, and the noble gorilla sat in glass cases. The largest display showed the White-Mantled Colobus, a group of forty long-haired, long-faced black and white monkeys in tree-tops, above what the museum artist had intended to be a valley some thousands of feet below. Like Church Fathers or Academicians, they sat, mournful and deliberating. Among them, the females took virtuous care of the young.

"They've confused the apes with the angels here, haven't they?" Nellie said.

"Above the fray," Sara said, "thinking only worthy thoughts."

"But actually," said Nellie, "probably beside themselves about the hominids grunting below, overtaking them in the natural stakes. And doing everything wrong, being 'cosmopolitan' and 'highly social.'"

"Drinking too much," said Sara. "Fiddling with reproduction."

130

"Breastfeeding too long," said Nellie, "oh, and betraying the greater vision of the larger brain."

"For what?" Sara asked. "All that grasping?"

"I don't know," said Nellie, "but they do, and the Abstract Expressionists knew."

"Your painters?" asked Sara.

Out of the monkey wing now, they walked past Klipspringers and Wapitis, the Spotted Skunk and Cacomistle, through the dark halls, lit only by the presentation of animals.

"It seems rather anthropomorphic this stuff, doesn't it?" Nellie asked Sara. "They're always in happy couples, like articles in *Vogue*. 'An evening with the Elks' over here. Sam Elk stands in front of his new home, a view of the Pasadena Country Club behind him. His wife Alison prepares a rare dinner at home: "I love to cook," she says, "but what with all the moving and surviving, I don't always get the time." ' Do you think," Nellie continued, "the animal world is so full of happy couples and proud homeowners, good mothers and responsible dads? Is that nature or the view of naturalists in 1910, or are they trying to make it palatable for us? They might have had cases displaying the cheetahs in domestic dispute, or Sam Elk caught in flagrante with the Elk next door."

"Or just the peril of life," said Sara, "they must have been a little terrorized by famine and predators."

"Did they suffer angst, do you think?" Nellie joked.

"Just terror," said Sara.

"But they look so happy here, peaceful, and confident, and upstanding."

"It's because they're dead," said Sara, "and stuffed."

131

"So they don't get depressed," Nellie said, not getting Sara's drift.

"They don't have to," Sara said, "they're already there."

Sunday afternoon had turned into Sunday evening by the time Nellie returned, alone, to her apartment. Not only were the Sara-feared signs of domestic bliss absent, so were most signs of life. The place had a mournful, neglected air about it, abandoned. Nellie sat down on the couch and thought how not to get depressed. There was no one to call at the moment. Everyone would be out somewhere. Laughing. Perhaps if she got really depressed she could start the housecleaning she had advised her sister. That would be something. Perhaps she should work, she had an interview to do next week, the catalog was going to be late as it was and she was going to make it later. She ought to work. She sat.

Next to her on the sofa was the answering machine with its little red light. Perhaps something had happened. She pushed the rewind button too far, the messages were days old, already answered or ignored: Rebecca, Melanie Howard, a party not attended, a dental secretary, a confirmation of a meeting at the office, and then a space with a lot of shy clicking off, bleeping and then at the end, like a flashlight in a tunnel, the only new sound among all the dead noises, the voice of Connaly, hypocritically apologizing, irritatingly seductive, but something alive.

THERE HAD BEEN WEEKS of delays, phone calls back and forth, explanations to Head of Publications, but now finally, Nellie was driving to East Hampton to interview her Abstract Expressionist critic. When Hugo left, a month ago, it was this picture of herself, sandal-shod in the VW, moving swiftly up the Long Island Expressway, that she'd had as sole projected image for the weeks ahead.

Now she drove, not as in imagination smoothly, nor as high point of her time alone, but as diversion from all the confusion around her, a clean, amoral act. Work had virtue in a Protestant culture, even work carried out in sandals, and it certainly had its purity, lying as it did outside the realm of Nellie's personal moral chaos.

But that wasn't quite true either, because in the past weeks, thanks to the business with Connaly, her work life had begun to show signs of deterioration, neglect, like an uncared-for husband. Please, Nellie said to herself, changing lanes anxiously as ever, no analogies. Still, all that recent business with Connaly had taken its toll. He had been a surprise to her, making her quieter, less smart, and quite a little confused. Almost as though escaping him, Nellie now drove in high gear towards the East.

There had been some fuss at the Museum as to whether

133

this trip was necessary, given that the catalog was going to be late already. They had finally compromised by allowing her the time off, if Nellie would pay for the gas. Otherwise the petty cash slips would need justification, but on aesthetic and philosophical grounds, because of who it was she was asking to see.

There had been two major critics of the movement. One, who in rather numerate fashion ("there are only three good painters," "the five pictures of 1952," etc.) had seen the thing as acting out a formalist necessity, progressing from one triumph to another along a predetermined course, measurable only by appearances; and the other one, Bateman, the one Nellie wanted to see, who, his enemies at the Museum held, didn't really care what the paintings looked like, as long as he could write, at passionate length, about what they meant.

The work of this man was thus held to be irrelevant to the aims of the present exhibition, which was to enable the public to see, without the accompanying period hysteria, what the pictures really looked like. But offering the public the smears and drips in "pure state" would, Nellie thought, be a disaster. They were to her like rabbit tracks in the snow, important not as tracks but as evidence of the rabbit. As appearance alone, the work would have only a weak hold on the mind.

But there was something else in Nellie's desire now to talk to Bateman. When she was calm she could see it, hanging separately from the professional and aesthetic question. It had to do with some analogy, merely sensed, between her own confusion and theirs, those growling painters of thirty years ago. For example, there was a picture by de Kooning, not considered good enough to use in the show, and rather a freak among his work, that had arrested Nellie. It was a portrait, in the figurative forties' style, recognizably of the artist, his head turned upwards, his face strained and confused, as if in laborious quest, a pilgrim making poor progress. Around him were abstract shapes, lines, bumps, vague and menacing, like the night terrors of children. Just a portrait of the artist with the background not bothered with, left abstract. Only the background had been exactingly painted and *rendered* abstract. The picture was called something like "Willem in the Wilderness" and had been painted at the point of the artist's career when his work had teetered between figurative and abstract. It was possible that the wilderness referred to was the aesthetic quandary, but it seemed to Nellie that the wilderness might be made of the lumps and shapes of de Kooning's life, things not quite seen, or else seen and not dared focused upon.

Of course Nellie at that moment felt like Willem, lost among all the things in her life that were undefined, blurry sensations triggered by thoughts of Connaly, of Hugo, of Sara, or else not yet readable, fragmented edges of things only partly remembered. But it wasn't that by itself, it was the fact that the artist had *made* his wilderness abstract that bothered her. If it was only the art-historical question, in the terms set at the time, i.e., should Bill go abstract, then it didn't interest her. But it seemed to Nellie that the picture wasn't about that, but about dread and not naming things, or not seeing them wholly and hence dreading them.

Certainly there was a connection between abstraction and hiding, and abstraction and confusion, but might there not also be a connection between abstraction and depression, that deadness of not feeling things, not focusing on other people, other acts, but sitting tightly among the sensations: Pollock's passions, Rothko's gloom, de Kooning's ambivalence?

There had been such a lot of caution in that movement. They really had been Cold War artists, lurking in bands, changing their names, having enemies, and hiding, always. Even the young Pollock's therapeutic drawings done voluntarily in hospital for his psychiatrist had shown not the private fantasies of the artist, but his artistic aspirations. His doctor had wanted the private symbols, Pollock had given him quotations from Picasso's "Guernica." And even now when you talk to them, wildly successful as some of them have been, it's the same, a constant mistrust and hostility, all that embedded paranoia.

But what were they so afraid of? Why did they say that only art could be the arena in which to act—as though all other arenas teemed with beasts that would kill? Where did it come from, the dread, and that word "risk"? What could you possibly risk by painting in wild ecstatic sweeps or drips of color? And yet that there was something terrible you had to admit, for the casualties had been horrific. Again, Motherwell's phrase ran in Nellie's head: "I belong to a generation that mainly killed itself, in one way or another."

The journey down to the self, the imprisonment in sensation had been fatal. Was it that, or was it nothing to do with the philosophy behind the art? Well, if anyone could tell her, Bateman could, what there had been about Abstract Expressionism that had undone so many.

· · · ·

136

And so much of it had happened here, under the sun, along the white beaches of the Hamptons, so much blind misery at the resort. Nellie drove her car past the Big Duck and the chichi shops of Bridgehampton till she got to the ornamental pond of East Hampton. Here she made a turn, driving almost instinctively as though not knowing where she was headed till she saw that she was up a long shaded avenue that arrived at the opening of Georgica Beach, between the ludicrously large clapboard and stucco houses of the American rich, not yet fully in force for the summer, for the season was barely two weeks old.

Once, many years ago, she and Sara and Rebecca and Louisa had lived in a guest cottage on one of these larger estates, the home of a wealthy connection of Louisa's, then between marriages and in need of recuperation. Nellie could not remember which outsize driveway had been theirs, which ostentatious lawn giving off which discreet lane. She drove slowly in the VW, picking up a sense of something in the shapes made by the road, the angle of this roof against these trees, the slope of a lawn.

Nor did Nellie remember well what kind of summer it had been. That had rather fused with other childhood summer memories, stays at a cousin's farm in Connecticut, Augusts in France and Scotland. But she remembered Louisa's long brown legs in white shorts, her Mexican sandals, and that under her hat, Louisa had smelled of sun oil and lemonade.

Someone must have been there looking after Sara; Nellie couldn't remember. She sort of remembered Rebecca, in teenage lumpiness and sulks, refusing to take herself to the beach, refusing to make friends. And then Nellie had been here since then with Hugo, but to different parts of the Hamptons. That was different, and something hadn't sunk in the way it had here, though really Nellie couldn't remember anything of that summer or where precisely it had been, nothing but a vague impression, entirely pleasant, of familiarity.

That was all really, just a sense that something good had happened along these roads, giving a special quality to its curves and lines, its relation to sea and horizon. Nothing but the familiarity of its serpentine crawl through the surrounding estates, which became in that instance a revelation to her, a suspension of all questions and a conviction that everything was out there, simply waiting to be experienced as good. Maybe one has just to relax and let go and see that it all really is rather all right, Louisa, Sara, Rebecca, Hugo, Connaly, all good. Goodness, said Nellie, what a little Pollyanna; this is not revelation, it is simply mood.

Nellie stopped the car in the area set aside for parking, and got out of her clothes in the car. As though in New York, she leaned over to lock the passenger seat door, then willing to put her Candidery to the test, left the car doors unlocked, the tape-recorder on the seat. She took, however, the car keys, and wrapped them in the towel.

When she was a child the waves had frightened her. Not so much as Sara who actually had to be dragged into the water and even then wouldn't let go of your hand, with the result that when a wave came you were likely as not knocked down and pulled under in the very manner that Sara had dreaded. For Nellie that was the exhilarating part. What was scary was when the sea was quiet, between the waves, and one could imagine what was out there, swimming slowly to shore. There would be a lull in the squeals of children on the beach, while the horizon divided the blue/gray haze from the black mass of the sea, and you felt the sluggish weight of undertow. The dread had been there, even at ten, as the linking space between the excitements of normal life, birthday parties at other children's houses, trips to movies, tears and tantrums with Louisa. Between the events of life, the "acts," a slow, black, sticky dread coming out of nowhere. And was *that* "real" or just mood?

A wave rolled in, and crashed, white against Nellie's legs, soaking her suit and for a moment catching her in simple body panic at the cold. She ran from the water to the towel, remembered the keys as they spilled out, caught them and wrapped the towel around her waist like a sarong. To dry out before meeting Bateman, she began to walk along the beach. There was no wind but the air by the sea was cold even in the sun. In a few weeks' time, farther down this beach towards Amagansett, where the AEs had once hung out, the place would be crowded with singles, not singles permanently alone but singles hoping to get coupled, beyond the imagining of those self-proclaimed solitaries, those white-bodied, drink-sodden painters that had once stumbled through the reeds and brought copies of *Art News* to their picnics.

Perhaps you could just choose these things, like clothes, choose to lie around brown and beautiful and happy or choose to sit apart, paint-spattered and stricken. Then what was it that had darkened Rothko's paintings, pursued Pollock into the trees, had battened on to Gorky long before the last events that led to his suicide, that had made up the paranoid style and talk of the Abstract Expressionist era? The critic would tell her.

139

Nellie got back in the car and put her dress over her still damp suit, her sandals on her feet. It was five o'clock. She turned the VW out of the parking lot, drove through the area of Georgica houses, up through Amagansett to Springs, the once blue-collar district where Bateman lived. De Kooning lived there too, near Pollock's old house and studio. It was as yet something of a backwater, becoming more desirable as the formerly glamorous areas of the Hamptons gave over to the tack and hustle of modern real estate ventures. Here was still, among the artists' and writers' residences, a strong hint of the old farming and fishing community, rougher roads than elsewhere, ungroomed lawns, uncollared dogs, gas stations and small general stores, a cemetery that held the famous dead: Stuart Davis, Jackson Pollock, Ad Reinhardt, Frank O'Hara, among the local dead: the Millers, Johnsons, and Stones. Bateman's house was a typical tree-surrounded cabin, to which, in the increasing prosperity of later life, had been added extensions and terraces with glass enclosures. The core of the house, into which Nellie now walked through an open door, was as it had been some thirty years ago when Bateman arrived with his wife and books from 10th Street: two small rooms off a large kitchen whose shelves held bottles of drink and dirty cooking pans.

Nellie stood inside the patch of sunlight calling into the center of the house. A deep low voice answered, followed by the figure of a handsome man in his early seventies, well over six feet tall, barrel-chested and brown from the sun. He was naked except for his khaki shorts which, together with his dignified bearing, gave him the look of a hero in a British prisoner-of-war film. In the winter Nellie had seen him once arriving at the Museum, in fur hat and

140

moth-eaten coat, a huge Tartar prince come to the capitol. Now he approached Nellie stiffly, stooped his silver head and shook hands.

"Boy, they're hiring them young at the Modern these days," Bateman said to her, "what are you, sixteen? Well, modern means modern I guess." His voice was a rich but fast quack, delivered from the side like Groucho Marx. "OK, so you're here," he said as she stood there, "nice to see you, come on."

He turned his back and led her into a large light-filled living-room. On the walls were hundreds of paintings, drawings, photographs, tributes and gifts from the artists. Bateman took what was evidently his chair, put a leg on the facing ottoman and made a gesture of "sit down" at her.

Nellie had brought with her a bottle of wine for their afternoon talk. It was part of her picture of this meeting, the two of them—the wise and the confused—drinking cold hock in the fading light of that early June evening. Of course the bottle was no longer cold. She offered it to him.

"Gee, thanks," Bateman said. "You stay there, I'll get glasses." It took him a while to get up, get to the kitchen, pull the cork and come back. Nellie's timing was off, she should have given him the wine before he sat. Bateman poured a glass for Nellie, handed it to her and sat down heavily in his seat. His own wine he drank all at once and put the empty glass on the floor beside his chair.

"It's not very cold, I'm afraid," said Nellie.

"It's OK. Well," he said abruptly, "what do you want to know?"

You couldn't just baldly ask. Nellie talked about the

141

progress of the show and about some of the paintings in the room where they were sitting. The critic laughed occasionally and watched her talking. There was a hint of impatience. Then Nellie asked a version of her question.

"Nah," Bateman said, "there were terrific times too, you know, parties, drinking. All that sad stuff is later, laid on for the establishment, you people. The art public likes their artists to suffer for them, get a little roughed up. Long before Van Gogh's ear. God knows, they help them when they can, and then of course when they're really down in the pit there's the occasional gladiatorial reward. Then you people go around doing shows and adjusting market values, puffing up the agony, which not only sells pictures, but gives a little frisson of merit to the curatorial acts. Sure the boys had fun. Painting's fun, for one thing, getting all splattered."

"But they talk about tragedy themselves," Nellie insisted, a little stunned. "When they talk it sounds like they're walking on egg-shells, that the structure of the world is going to come to pieces at any moment."

"Everyone has a bad day," said Bateman.

"But it's in the art."

"*Aggie,*" Bateman shouted to his wife through the open door. Nellie had a wild notion that he was going to have her removed. Instead, he told her, "Everything's in the art. I quote de Kooning, 'Art is like a soup, everything's in it.' "

"But there's such a burden on the self in it," Nellie said, "performance and sensibility are everything." Nellie was nervous about Aggie. If she didn't come, he would shout again.

"Well, they had to paint something." Bateman leaned

forward and looked at his watch. "And if they'd been painting nudes, sweetie, you'd never be putting on this show, and I'd never have written about them."

"*Aggie,*" he shouted. A thin unhappy voice called back.

"But why?" Nellie had fought at the Museum to get this far: she would ask.

"Because," he sighed, "the modern painter is the painter of modern life, and modern life is not nudes, it's . . ."

"What?"

"Ambiguity, negative capability, and incapacities. No certainties in modern life."

"And so," Nellie paraphrased the critic's well-known words, "unable to act with certainty in modern life, the modern painter takes his capacity to act where it still is possible, in his painting. Painting has become the arena in which to act."

"That's right," said Bateman.

Aggie had arrived. Nellie could not see her; she was hovering behind the door. "Bring me a Scotch will you," he asked her. "This lady's got wine."

"And painting is the last act of which modern man is capable?" Nellie went on, desperately ingratiating.

"No, there's suicide too, ask the French."

Aggie returned with the Scotch. You could only see her forearm with the drink, plump and brown and freckled.

"When do we eat?" Bateman snapped. Aggie said something—Nellie couldn't quite hear. Maybe they ate now? She moved forward, "But isn't there a connection between art that places such a burden on the self and the philosophy that says nothing else is possible but art and suicide?"

143

"No."

"What about Rothko?"

"Rothko was a vulgarian. He knew it and tried to paint himself *out* of the picture, that's why he killed himself, tried to wipe himself off the canvas with all those pure colors, all his moaning about God and tragedy and fate. You know he had a place out here at Louse Point and we went to see him one day. He came out of the garden. He was standing there with a broken spade and these ticks all over his legs. I said, Mark, what the hell you doing? You better get those goddam bugs off, you're gonna be sucked dry. That was the tragedy of nature for Rothko, the guy was a clutz in the garden."

"But isn't that the same," Nellie went on, "as saying there's no connection between the world and the painter, they don't know how to do it, connect with it, care for it, garden it, live in it anymore?"

"That's right," said Bateman, relaxing into self-quotation, "connection is no longer possible. Still possible probably in Europe, but I haven't been over for twenty years. They have a society there, anyway, used to. Here there is no society, only crowds. And no conversation, either, just chat. And if you want to know what all these philosophical painters talked about between masterpieces, the answer is probably cars and baseball. Probably what you people talk about when you're not smoking pot."

"But, I don't . . ."

"Oh yeah," Bateman said, smiling at himself, "you work at the Museum, you probably talk about significance and authenticity. Well, we used to talk about other things, you know, who was winning the Series."

144

"The Series?" Nellie sat back in her chair; the damp of her bathing suit was going to come through her dress.

"Sure." Bateman finished his drink and set it down. Nellie thought that was the signal for the end, but he roused himself and said, "Listen."

Nellie sat forward one last time.

"When Franz Kline died in sixty-two I was out here. The boys decided to do a memorial kind of thing. So the ones that were getting it together asked me if I'd do a talk. I said sure. Well, I sat down to write it and I loved that bastard but I just couldn't think of a damn thing to say. So I called Bill over and I said, Bill, you and Franz were pretty tight, tell me something about him, really about him that I can say on whatever day the memorial thing was. So Bill thinks and he says nothing and he's very sad, and I'm sad, and then he says, 'Jesus, you knew Franz. He was one hell of a third baseman.' "

"Was that all?" Nellie said.

The critic's face darkened.

"I mean," Nellie said, "did you use that?"

"Sure, that's what I said," said Bateman, "that was all you had to say about Franz."

ON A THURSDAY EVENING in the latter part of June, Nellie sat with Connaly watching *La Règle du jeu* in the airless art cinema on Bleecker Street. All around her in the dark, the heavy faces turned upwards towards the light, like the prisoners in *Fidelio*. The film they were watching was one of Hugo's favorite films, Connaly said it was one of his favorite films, and so they had gone, post-intercourse, and pre-dinner to watch what Renoir had made of a subject much on their minds, or much on Nellie's mind, the subject being adultery. Nellie's first notion of keeping the thing going by means of two planes of consciousness was not working out. In the past weeks, not taking this old lover seriously as a new lover, she had watched herself with a certain horror, and as it continued, with a certain detached tolerance, never doubting for a moment that it would fail by its own feebleness to last until the scheduled return of her husband.

That return was now some two weeks off and nothing was winding up as planned. Furthermore, the two planes, or rather the two characters strapped in to pilot them, naughty Nellie with Connaly, and serious, sensitive Nellie with Hugo, were not keeping decently apart. And the difficulty of not letting the two selves collide was only the hardest of the maneuvers involved in the adultery. Those other dissimulations, the bedroom farce stuff—so gaily rendered in the aforementioned and ironically (by Connaly) and at times uncomfortably (by Nellie) watched film —had been mostly, thanks to Hugo's stay in Africa, spared her. Rebecca was beginning to ask with sarcasm about Nellie's suddenly increased workloads, and to sit up a bit, when on occasion they met at Louisa's, at various signs of Nellie's being physically attended to—the normal widow's droop being suspiciously absent. Yet it would suit Rebecca to believe that the husbandless life could be by itself refreshing, and really Rebecca was clearly more and more taken up by her quandaries with Robert. It was evident from hints dropped to Nellie that the big questions were being asked, at least by Rebecca, of Rebecca. Robert had only to begin saying aloud what Rebecca was saying to herself for the whole thing to become real, and a crisis. Sara had seen nothing or said nothing, and Louisa would always assume the best. True, there had been some minor notice paid by the building people, as yet no eyebrows, only a sense conveyed that the Christmas tip would need to accommodate discretion. But there had been one stupidity, the morning a week ago when the cleaning lady had come in to find Nellie in bed, having overslept, and beside her, the sleeping, sodden, undisguisably male mass of Connaly. Confused and upset, the woman had shut herself into the kitchen until they'd left, Nellie hushing Connaly and feeling the betrayal, not of Hugo, but of that tenderest enquirer after Hugo.

And yet, the chaos of this affair was not here, along the protruding edges of the action, but more centrally present in Nellie's thinking about the two men and herself with them. There was beginning to be a change in her manner

147

of seeing them, a change in their very visibility. Over her sense of Hugo, Nellie felt a kind of creeping fog, while the oddest things about Connaly were coming into focus and beginning to attach themselves to Nellie's image, both when she saw him and when she thought of him, something to do with his energy and directness, the ease with which he recognized and followed his instincts. It wasn't in the least a question of comparing Hugo and Connaly, there was no comparison, she had chosen Hugo years ago, and with a reasoning anyone could understand. Connaly was her old redneck sweetheart, young America, suitable for teenage loving and nothing more, or only a little more. But the fact was that Connaly, whether through his own virtues or his mere continuing presence was beginning to have a certain reality which properly belonged—or so Nellie had fondly (in both senses of that word) believed—to Hugo alone.

And Hugo was to her treacherous mind, or was it merely an extraordinary shortness of memory, beginning to take on the properties of the element he had last vanished into. She had had one postcard from him in all this time, of male warriors with naked buttocks, covered in dried red mud (or was it blood?), crouching around a dog-eared zebra. It had said that Tony and Anna were fine and that Tanzania was hot. It had been post-marked an impressively few six days before it arrived. It had failed entirely to convey to Nellie a sense of her husband, the fact of his absence from New York or his presence in Africa.

It was really pretty bad. Hugo had been gone such a little time compared with the months and months he'd been with her, and Nellie actually had trouble picturing what he looked like. Of Connaly there beside her, breathing through his mouth in the darkened cinema, she could tell without looking how the light moved in the space between eye and cheekbone, how the skin colors changed with his emotion. She could probably choose the paints necessary to match them. But of the beloved husband, it was horrifyingly the case that Nellie, if you'd asked her then, would fail to say with certainty the shade of Hugo's eyes, the precise shape of his nose.

That is not to say she would not recognize him when he got back—she wasn't mad exactly—but that his appearance on return would surprise her, as it always did, with the little something that was different from the way she'd imagined it. Inevitably, Hugo would be thinner or paler or younger looking than she'd anticipated. It was as though literally, as much as figuratively, her marriage had depended on her not looking too closely. After that first looking, general, cool, appraising, and after the intense lover's looking, transforming, sanctifying, there had been again the cool appraisals, curious, friendly, unarmed. But mostly there had been marital looking, which is not looking at all, except for signs of trouble, signs of health, pulse-taking or else tracking—the radar of conjugal defense.

Yet Nellie knew that Hugo's coming back would begin to diminish Connaly's reality, and reestablish proper proportions: the full-statured life-sharing husband and the minor fling, instead of what it now seemed, the larger-than-life, all-thought-and-body-engaging lover and the distant husband, off somewhere and no bigger than a speck on Nellie's horizon. How her disloyalty manifested itself in near-sightedness! Or was she simply a case of the long-by-her disbelieved stereotype: the heartless betraying

woman? Was the proximity of the man all that was necessary to transform what was minor into what was major, or
was there something else in this business with Connaly—
unmysterious as he apparently was, and unnovel as he
should have been? And was there something else in her
treachery to Hugo, a message that as long as this affair
were kept secret would never be delivered? And why was
she fretting about all of it so ceaselessly, unable to sit back
and enjoy the trumping as a simple act of nature, a forgiv-
able deviation from the longed-for but seldom attained
moral rectitude, the way these happy and charming
French people seemed to, and with what ease, and with
what innocence, Watteau. Sit back, Nellie, Nellie said to
herself, enjoy the film.

The problem was that it couldn't really be so fine for
her to be doing if it weren't fine for Hugo. And it would
not be that. In such matters, Nellie's sense of fairness, not
to mention of liberty and fraternity went one way, her
insecurities another. Egalitarian in principle, she hoped to
get away with autocratic practice. OK for her, but outra-
geous for Hugo. Because what if now as she sat in this
dark pit of art, the amatory juices just ebbing into a pleasant dampness, a very faint soreness making itself the not
inappropriate background sensation for the Renoir, Hugo
were warmly engaged with some firm-fleshed Nubian, offered to him like an after-dinner cigar by his Tanzanian
host, or with some honey-colored planter's wife of roseate
nipples and Rhodesian speech? How then would Nellie
feel? She would feel, wouldn't she, outclassed and over-
thrown, threatened, not only in the manner of the first
lady of the harem asked to embrace the newest bride, but
threatened logically? Because she would be asked to con-

sider once again whether marriage, with its built-in guarantee of emotional boredom, with its almost guarantee of sexual deception was such a good idea when there was single life available, with *its* guarantees of sexual and emotional boredom, of course, and spiritual degradation and so on, both to be weighed and considered and compared until in the end all deviations from the ideal are just forgiven in exchange for the pleasures of forgetting. And perhaps it really isn't such a good idea to wake up all these questions all the time, but better to enjoy the peaceful sleep of the soundly married.

In the seat next to Nellie, Connaly stirred. Some instinct told him she was, in her thoughts, away from him, and he brought his arm over her shoulder to restore his presence in her world. The waft from that gesture inside the stuffy theater, his sweat mingling with the wool of his tweed jacket (this Californian's idea of dress for a New York June) returned him to her, together with a sharp sense of their lovemaking two hours ago. How could Hugo compare with the strength of that, triggered so simply, so *un*metaphysically by Connaly's odors? And fancy their arousing so much affection in Nellie when to anyone else—the girl on Nellie's left, for instance, face muscles minutely tensing, head fractionally averting, they must be irritating—an offense and interruption of the loss of self in this airy sweet-smelling film. But to Nellie, sinking happily into that odiferous moist tweed, physical ease. The flesh was so willing, and the spirit so weak.

Yet a deal had been made, that Hugo's behavior should not disturb Nellie's peace and vice versa. If Hugo knew about Connaly he'd be crushed and unhappy, all sorts of goblins would tear from the earth. There'd be tantrums

and tears, and all sorts of ancient, dusted-off recrimina-
tions. Or there'd be worse, that acceptance of it all, life
and expectation put one gear lower, patience and courtesy
and silence where there used to be trusting babble. Or else
a deep misery, with which they would go to bed, back
against back, every cell in the other's body sensibly, per-
ceptibly altered, hard and hostile, and that awful waking,
at first in ignorance and then with the increasing knowledge that this day and the days to come would all be
different from the days that had set one's habit of waking
as it had been, secure in one's life and with one's reason for
getting out of bed.

Or there might after enough of that even be divorce,
not just the long awful procedure and the starting again—
that could, Nellie supposed and had read, be improving in
some girlscouty way—but the terrible sentence that one
should never again be with Hugo, never go to a movie like
this one with him, never share a meal, never catch him
just sitting on the edge of the bed trying to unwork a
knot in his shoelace, deep in concentration and secure,
anxious only about the knotted lace, at home with himself
because of what he had with Nellie.

That was the exchange in question: that tiny happiness,
like a film-still remembered, requiring no participation,
nothing but a certain sensibility, for what Connaly offered, not to be thrown away lightly—well, what in Nellie's life was ever thrown away lightly?—a physical happiness, at present, an extraordinary well-being in bone and
flesh, though it left, did it not, the heart untouched? But
it was the animal birthright, a precarious dancing on the
moment, the animal terror, perhaps, the animal joy.

Just now it had been extraordinary. They had done

152

what the occasion demanded and lost themselves in sex. That is, Connaly had lost all those old selves and present limits of his Connalyness, and Nellie had lost hers—they had become nothing but, nothing less than, male and female, the abstractions themselves.

It was as if Nellie had accomplished a long escape from all those ties which bound her to her real world, her age and her race, her parentage and education, had shed along with her clothes that evening all the defining and material realities that had, like the tiny ropes on the vast body of Gulliver, kept her prisoner in an alien place. With Connaly she had left this behind, and in her nakedness found, or rather become, another world, an infinitude of body, created for and presently existing only for that other body, which was Connaly, likewise freed, sprung from the prison of his daily self, with its shackling wants and habits, to become simply an energy and a direction and an element for Nellie's universe. Together, the one enabling the other, they had abandoned the world they knew: the sheets and their white folds, the dust on the floor, the sounds of the elevators in the hall, the cat padding outside the door, the softening, then hallowing light of early evening; and they had gone through their bodies so far away from their bodies and at the same time so far inside their flesh that each had become a microcosm for the other—a vast realm of miraculous growth and explosion that parodied nature and natural time, like a Disney film, in which the slowest, quietest flowering appears as a kind of fireworks display, fit for the music of John Philip Sousa.

But afterwards, afterwards all gravity returned. All heaviness and futility and selfhood returned, no trace of the recent miracle flight, except the whine of the body, the affectionate turning away, the overriding need for sleep.

Rebecca would call it good sex or remarkable sex and be grateful for it. And Nellie too, merely thinking in this remote fashion of what Rebecca would call it felt the memory and body gratitude for what had happened and might happen again. Yet somewhere she rebelled against it—the loss of her will and her individuality. She loved herself more, perhaps that was it. If so, she would never really be free, from her self and the doom of her need to know always where she was and how she'd got there, what it would cost to remain and how she might control what was going to happen. And yet she did not then care about such notions of freedom, she did not care if she could not be an instinct-following animal or a star-shooting flower. She did need to be herself, inside the little space that Hugo left her.

It would be clear to anyone if they had come from what Rebecca would have called incredible sex that this film was not about erotic power. For the people in the film retained every speck of the character they had when fully dressed, and all the charms of the self—except the poor gamekeeper in the throes of jealousy, who was beside himself. Nellie rather approved of that notion of civilization, blasted as it was by the shotgun at the end of the film. She too, she supposed, wanted a world where people smiled and flounced and sniveled in and out of each other's lives, with no disasters, no despair, no inalterable consequences. And if that were to be had at the cost of all manner of apocalyptic insight, so much the better. For what was she to do or Connaly to do with the knowledge that they could act upon each other as fire and water, heaven and hell? And what possible use could be made of such knowledge, in the rest of their lives, their sitting in subway cars, restaurants, to their office lives, to the norms of their conversation? The consequence of revelation was change; one might have to live one's life differently if such things were to be taken seriously, or if one allowed one's mind to accept the wisdom of the body.

Perhaps it's not even possible to prolong revelation; if so, she and Connaly, and probably dozens of others in this audience would be sitting in a state of grace, transformed by the blessings of the body, lifted from the clod of their normalcy, like the bare-footed laborer angels on Tiepolo's ceilings. No longer would they crave popcorn or cigarettes, nor shift in their seats or cough or squint to read the white-on-white lettering of the subtitles. No, best to let sex exist like a gap in real life, to be a place like an airplane is to those in terror of flying, a place always the same, triggering accumulated memory when there, always forgotten as soon as possible upon leaving. Because the other way is too dangerous. You might not live your life, but endure pining for such release, like an addict, like a mystic craving the light.

And how unreliable the whole thing is after all, a bad place to seek salvation, among such undependables: desire, maleness, femaleness, the whole thing that seems to be as guaranteed as a stable of cows and bulls, a bag of grunts dipped into when the lust is on, and not as it is, a fragile structure put together with precision instruments, where no guarantees obtain, where no experiments can be repeated, not with the very same person under what appear to be the very same conditions, not with the best intentions or the greatest will that it should be again as it once was. Even so, it comes and goes, as though it really were a kind of grace.

It is peculiar that the French are credited with so much wisdom in matters of sex. Or maybe matters of love, of which sex used formerly to be only one part. In America, or rather in New York, to which her experience was limited, it seemed to Nellie to be the other way around—all that love chat was part of a foreplay to be culminated by orgasm, forgotten after use, and hardly taken seriously at the time. That great American thrust, its manifest destiny, was towards orgasm, covering whole continents of sensibility on the way, ignoring it like so much landscape, to be littered as much as looked at. In this, Connaly had been the real thing, pioneering through trackless wastes of Nellie's presence in bed, his little Davy Crockett hat brushing her brow, until, having proceeded stage by stage —a little stagecoach by himself—he'd arrive, the big country! He got them there all right, and always on time, a little iron horse on his track, but all the other "stuff," the courtship, the talk, the lover's sensibilities, seemed to Nellie to have been feigned, deemed necessary in Connaly's experience, to cover territory where women were concerned. There had been the merest lip-service paid to the mysteries of the thing. Mystery was for the impotent ones. Connaly knew the whole thing to be studiable and performable. A little like Jackson Pollock, really, wanted to "see" the emotion, have the feelings right out there, visible. And there was a case for such simplicity. Certainly the French made rather too much of the secrecy with their little perfumes and boxes, zippers and nattiness, a great fuss about underwear and semiology. Just the opposite of the Connalys, the French wanted everything to be other than it seemed. Pouf! whip the linen from an elegant table and a worm-eaten board is revealed; whip the apparent meaning from a sentence and the history, direction and multiple intent can be seen; pouf! whip away the nun's black habit, lace knickers, and underneath those, ohn-hohn, just ask Maurice Chevalier.

It was in Paris that Nellie and Connaly had first come to make "the beast with two backs," under the shadow of the gargoyles of Notre Dame. Nellie had known that that was what they were going to Paris to do. Until that moment there had been all that yes-no, yes-no business, in the time-honored convention, Nellie like everyone else having been obliged to play the cardboard role, coy virgin to Connaly's bleeding courtier. "In Paris," she had said again and again, in order to gain time in the months after the crossing. Eventually, after Christmas, Nellie had lied to Louisa, Connaly had lied to his parents and they had gone off to the trysting place. The flat belonged to a colleague of the father of Nellie's good friend at school, the same kind father offered by life prematurely who one weekend when Connaly and Nellie had come to visit his daughter, had given them a single room with a single bed, long before unified bedding was wanted, and they had lain both nights sleepless, Connaly in a fit of adolescent longing checked by adolescent honor, Nellie in pure dread, not so much of the thing she did not know how to do as of her host's discovery that in his house, befriended by his daughter, was no sophisticate of seventeen, but a New York provincial, unworthy of his liberal views or sense of paternal style.

157

But after Christmas, and in Paris, the chips were all to be cashed in. Nellie went off with a French dictionary and what the English call a Dutch cap, and with her friend's instruction that you simply had to lie there "like a cow, the bloke has to figure it out."

But Nellie was so inadequate, even to lying there. It was impossible to keep still or quiet. Instead, throwing to the winds all hopes for the dignity of the thing, she had, freezing in her rosy flesh, talked a blue streak, acutely aware that there should have been more of her here and less of her there—though how much more embarrassed she might have been had her body been perfect! Better not to be irresistible when what you want is to be resisted, for him to go away, in fact, and leave you forever a child, advanced in mind and perfectly content to think the mind all there was of the world.

Her mind she insisted on, dragged in at every corner of their first uncovered meeting, talk, talk, joke, joke, her poor inadequate weapon against his desire. But Connaly soldiered on, invincible to her trumpeting, spread her nervous legs and forced his way, rudely indeed, where no man had been before. There was no pain and no pleasure, nothing but eventually her silence, relief in that silence on his part, relief in his final inactivity on hers. Afterward, they lay together dozing, more in nervous than physical exhaustion, while the evening bells of Notre Dame bonged the sacred hour, and a little flow of blood signaled the event.

In the mornings they went to the Louvre, walking up the steps in the dust-moted light, past the Winged Victory and its clumps of admirers, up to the huge marble landing where they chose their direction by their mood.

Sixteenth century if they were feeling heroic, early nineteenth if they wanted to be moved, Rembrandt if they were homesick—Rembrandt reminded them of the Upper West Side. The Rubens rooms they passed through at their own peril, for the paintings tended to depress; the scale of the things—the frames as much as the torsos—acted like a night full of stars to convince them of insignificance. Somehow their own coupling now past the terror stage, was so paltry next to that, their own beginning sense of each other so weakly next to the evidence of those grand passions, those abductions and outrages, tragic recognitions and godly possessions.

But, happily, there were Titians and Veroneses and the women of Ingres, perfect and undisturbable, whom Nellie loved and Connaly found cold and heavy and mockable, so that Nellie thereafter went only alone to pay homage there to paintings that paid homage to some as yet unrecognized principle in herself, perhaps only an evocation of the solitary nature of her sex.

And then, after the sight of so much coupling in impasto, so many breasts bared to swords, so many thighs caught up in the folds of immaculately rendered, soon to be rumpled, sheets, of so many eyes cast imploringly to heaven or to torso-buckled conquerors, home they would go to their own draperies and bedclothes, and with their own pink breasts and brown eyes, to unknowingly parody what they had seen in that place.

It became everything, the "lovemaking." They lived for it those three weeks in Paris, Connaly in some adolescent rapture that he was at last doing it, Nellie in a kind of inertia and because she knew then so little of what she was meant to expect. The setting confused her so that she thought whatever was wrong was her. Still, it went on, in the afternoon, when the orange light of the Paris winter came through the old windows on to the sheets of the bed, and they would sleep long hours until dinner at the Greek tabac below. Or after dinner, when they were drunk and full and it all seemed part of the same orgy of matter, wine or steak or Connaly, all an invading and enveloping element, smothering, no breath apart from this drunken sex, no sensation, no thought apart from desire and satiety, when her head swum under the alcohol breath of Connaly and her legs twisted in the coarse sheets. Or morning sex, long before the patches of light had come together to make the day, when the giant stirred, half of him still owned by sleep, half belonging with consciousness to Nellie, self-given, unasked for but dedicated. That early morning sex came closest to love, it was gentle and accommodating and tentative. If Nellie could have loved him at all, it would have been then, when he, a little removed by his sleep was closest to her, a little removed by her ignorance, her sense that something crucial was missing, her need for the time to find it.

Later, in England, as it went on, she grew to know that she hated him, and yet not know that there was any reason to stop. It was too much and too little: too much sex and too little love, too much of Connaly and his weight and force and ingenuity that became later a kind of desperation because he wanted her to surrender. Instead, while they were making "love," she learned how to watch him, keeping herself apart and watching his performance, for that is what it became, with high-diving and dipping and going under without air, and it was genuinely impressive, but it moved her not at all. Nellie did not know, how could she? She didn't even guess that the feelings of detachment, fraudulence, of a faint imposition, weren't what they all felt, all the women she had known, what Louisa felt, what Rebecca felt, what Sara and she were meant to feel. How could she know, from what she'd read, what she'd seen in museums—the courtesans of Goya or Manet or Matisse—that there was more to it than the thrill of power over someone else? That much she could see was attractive—that need of the other for oneself—and it was perfectly possible that the whole point of the thing, the whole secret, the pivot of the fuss was the thrill of seeing that desire in the other. Long before orgasm, Nellie had had the thrill of narcissism. For does not Titian's Venus lie naked in simple adoration of herself, and was not Nellie with Connaly simply and correctly doing the same? Real mating, real equality and connection with that opposite sex, that wasn't even a hinted possibility during the course of Nellie's first affair.

Then what was she doing with him now, when it had all been so constantly wrong even before it became loathsome? And how had she managed to get over that bridge to him, and she had, this very evening? Was she trying to show him that someone else had saved her, that she had been freed? She had been. She had loved others. She had loved Hugo.

But still, what was she doing with him? Would she, like the heroine of the film, have her interlude and return to her husband, the peace and quiet of the *réglé* life? As if forgetting that the carnage and chaos, the birds and aviators blasted to earth, gamekeepers and poachers dismissed, mechanical toys and château china broken, were all the exploded debris of a false life led inside an alien world.

Still, in the film there were servants to pick up the mess. Who would there be for that if Nellie lost Hugo?

Well, nothing would happen, would it? That was why she had chosen to have her liaison with an ex-lover so safe, so previously had and unloved that even these bedroom triumphs of his were unthreatening, remaining inside the quite limited arena of his power to surprise. Once again, thought Nellie, a coward, even in adultery, calculating the damage, too cautious for broken china, or simple inconvenience, or less simple, Sara's kind of terror. Then was Nellie bound to Hugo by nothing more noble than fear? Well then, she should give him up and find—if it exists— an uncalculated, unmeasured love.

NELLIE HAD SEEN REBECCA only briefly since their meeting at the Sherry Netherland, and was now surprised by the changed appearances of both Rebecca and her apartment. The latter was tidier than usual; all the little *bibelots* had been cleared off the table tops and the mantelpiece. From the bookshelves, the miniature vases with dried flowers, the art postcards, the tiny, gold-framed photographs, the pieces of cloth and glass that had stood between the eye and the severe tomes of Rebecca's law-dominated library were gone, swept away in a puritanical purge. Here, Nellie thought, was Robert's influence, or perhaps, Rebecca, herself, having "got" Robert, had decided that the softening touches and feminine lures were no longer needed. Or perhaps, since nothing so self-conscious was really attributable to Rebecca, Nellie had simply arrived in the middle of a cleaning. Rebecca herself certainly looked that way, with strands of hair drooping down her damp white neck, her makeup smudged, her purple silk kimono flapping open now and again over Rebecca's astounding white thighs as they crossed the room and disappeared into the corridor just after Nellie arrived. "Just coming," Rebecca called as she moved, "take some coffee. It's hot. How are you? I'll be out in a minute."

163

"You've cleared everything away," Nellie called after her.

"It was all catching dust," Rebecca said, as she came back into the room, holding her kimono shut in front of her. "It had to go. It was beginning to feel like someone's attic. And there's more space now."

Nellie sat down on the couch that used to be littered with silk-covered pillows, transforming Rebecca's flat into an Arab brothel, and came up against a bare wall.

"This is a bit functionalist for you, isn't it?" Nellie said, moving to the edge of the sofa. "Well, you're looking well." Rebecca smiled a little smile to herself, but said nothing.

Rebecca *was* looking well. It was frightening what a difference the past weeks had made. Rebecca's flesh, even under the old makeup, positively glowed with good treatment and self-love. "Is Robert here?" Nellie suddenly asked. Rebecca nodded, in pride and modesty, like a new mother cat.

"Sorry to disturb you," said Nellie. "I just wanted to drop Louisa's present off before your lunch today."

"You said on the phone, no disturbance, Nellie. It's nice to see you. What did you get Mother?" Rebecca held out her hand for the unwrapped box.

"Six weeks late and no paper, I hope she'll accept it."

"Good God." Rebecca held the elaborate and flimsy black nightgown under her chin. "Is this what sixty-year-old ladies get given these days?"

"Only the sexy ones. Do you think it's too much?"

"Robert, look what Nellie's got for Mother's sixtieth birthday," Rebecca said as Robert appeared before them, completely dressed and shining, like a man on his way to work.

"Good morning," said Nellie, "sorry to interrupt your Sunday."

"Good morning, Nellie," said Robert. "Yes, that is rather distinguished."

"But for Mother?" Rebecca laughed.

"I would say that was an entirely appropriate tribute from one female descendant. Your mother is a very lovely, sexy woman, with three like daughters."

"Well, what did you get her?" Nellie asked Rebecca.

"Champagne and perfume," said Rebecca. "Not very imaginative."

"But the same idea, really, homage to the sexual powers."

"Conferred upon her daughters," said Robert, smiling.

"Why, Robert," said Rebecca, "how do you know?"

"I can see," said Robert. And to Nellie, "Did you bring the paper?"

"No," said Nellie, "sorry."

"Have some coffee," said Rebecca, already in the kitchen to get it. Robert said neither yes nor no, but took the coffee when it came like a man to whom deference is due. Rebecca brought him in turn a small bowl of sugar, a spoon, an ashtray, and a heated donut on a plate. Each item was delivered with a certain anxious gesture and a peculiar affability, the manner of a new restaurant owner waiting on a table. Nellie had never seen her sister so self-effacing before, and while it was a little disturbing, she could not help regarding Robert with a new respect. It was extraordinary how his sexual authority had transformed her sister. But Nellie didn't quite like to see it, as

165

though she were intruding on the intimacy it derived from, and she was relieved when Robert eventually left.

When he was gone, Rebecca sat where she was, regarding Nellie somewhat sheepishly as though aware that her sister had witnessed her subservience. At the same time, her look implied that if asked she would say that such obsequiousness was a small amount to pay for so much well-being. Rebecca was, evidently, fully consciously happy. Whatever Nellie might think of the means that got her there, considered politely for old time's sake, of course, it mattered nothing compared with the transforming power of that.

When it was clearly no longer possible not to mention Robert, Nellie asked, "He doesn't work Sundays does he? I hope it's not because of me that he's off."

"No, of course not," Rebecca said. "I wasn't going to take him with me to Mother anyway. It sort of confuses the issue—of Sara and him. Jeopardizes the therapeutic relationship." Robert's jargon. Rebecca was gradually swallowing the whole man, slowly, like a boa constrictor, but one day the two people would merge. And there was a tiny show of defiance in it, together with pride, the sort that isolates one female from another when she has "got" a man.

But bravado wasn't necessary with Nellie, and ten minutes after Robert had left them, Rebecca returned to her former nature, back to the sisterhood, back to the old conspiracy of two women, or, in any case, of Rebecca with Nellie. She smiled thus two smiles at once, the smile of her success and the smile of her understanding of what that success amounted to in the eyes of another, well-wishing but un-besotted, a smile that admitted that Robert was not perfect and, at the same time, that that fact no longer mattered.

Rebecca got up to get more coffee and to break the moment. As she passed the fireplace, she paused to regard herself in the mirror over the mantel. Nellie watched the split-second of vanity as Rebecca looked, unconsciously setting her features in a moue—lips pressed forward, eyes sulky—that vanished as soon as the rhythm of Rebecca's stride took her past the image of herself on her way to the kitchen. But Nellie had seen it, and knew what it said about how well Robert loved her sister, had managed to overpower that sense of ugliness that women poorly loved drag about with them like a dead cat. That was what Rebecca's look in the mirror conveyed, a banished self-loathing, the gift of the magic lover, and not that other thing, the anxious checking in the mirror that the ugliness is as yet hidden. It seemed to Nellie that Rebecca by looking at herself merely reminded herself that Robert looked at her with love and pleasure.

There was a sanctity now about Rebecca's apartment, with all that love and sexual gratification bouncing off the walls that made Nellie feel, even with Robert gone, that she intruded.

"I should leave you," she said to Rebecca.

"Why?" Rebecca took Nellie's cup to refill it. "I haven't got to be at lunch till one. Stay, please, how are you anyway? I haven't seen you in ages." And thus Rebecca leapt over the obstacle of her happiness with Robert to invite Nellie back into her thoughts.

"Have you heard from Hugo," she said, "when's he getting back?"

"In about a week," Nellie said, though he might stay

167

longer. He hadn't written, but he never did. Yes, she wanted to see him. Nothing, really, mostly work, and so on.

Then, rather suddenly, as though after a decision, Rebecca said that she thought she and Robert might get married. She sat up a little, as though to take whatever blow Nellie's response might be. "He isn't perfect, I know."

"No," said Nellie. She was going to say that didn't exclude him from the rest of the world, but Rebecca interrupted her, "You don't think that matters?" she said.

"What *I* think doesn't matter," said Nellie, "What do you think?"

"I think it doesn't matter." Rebecca was rather cheerful that this was over. "Anyway," she went on, "we can always divorce if it doesn't work out."

"No," said Nellie suddenly, "and if you mean that, you mustn't bother to marry."

Rebecca gave an irritated sigh. "How old-fashioned you are, Nellie. Well, I suppose you are right. It's a rather large undertaking, though."

"Yes," Nellie smiled. "But it's either that or nothing."

"There are plenty of other ways," said Rebecca. She had thirty-eight years of "nothing" to defend to her married sister.

"I don't mean marrying, I mean really taking on the other person. Otherwise there really is nothing, black holes and self."

"Goodness," said Rebecca, "I'd no idea the risk I was running."

"You didn't run any risks; it's now you start. Seriously, Rebecca, I do think so, don't mock."

"Sorry."

"You know my Abstract Expressionists are always talking about risk. Well, at some point it was declared that the canvas was the arena in which to act. That's not true, other people are. Robert lets you connect with the world."

"But I'm here already."

"Not always, are you?"

"Yes."

"Well, Hugo's my arena."

"Always?"

"No, but that's the sad part."

"But you're describing a rather hideous dependency. What if Hugo dies, or Robert, you're saying the world is going to disappear."

"Well, it has for Sara, hasn't it?"

"But I wasn't, am not, Sara, nor you. This is nonsense, Nellie."

"But you were looking for Robert, weren't you? You never really said, I'm OK, perfectly balanced as I am, all by myself?"

"From time to time, sure."

"And how did that feel?"

"What do you mean?"

"Did it really feel like balance or like despair?"

"I don't think like either," said Rebecca, but she wasn't really able to remember the first state, so wrapped was she in this new one. Still, she said, "No, I'm sure I was perfectly OK thinking I might remain single. God knows, I was single a very long time. No despair."

"Well, that is not the way I remember it," said Nellie, "and you should see yourself now, little Miss Lazarus."

"Oh, come on," said Rebecca.

169

"No, really, Rebecca."

"You have, you know, a rather perverse way with a compliment. Anyway, I suspect you are merely missing Hugo. But, for God's sake, your life didn't stop just because he went away, did it?"

"He's not really away. And I am not, Rebecca, merely pining, thanks."

"No? After six weeks I would be."

"I didn't mean that."

"You're so old-fashioned, Nellie," said Rebecca, laughing, "I'd no idea."

"Oh Christ," said Nellie.

For a minute, Nellie smoked her cigarette, then she said, "There's just one thing, Rebecca."

"What?" She was almost laughing at her.

"Don't let Robert swamp you or take you over. It happens."

"All right, Nellie, I'll be careful."

"It happens because we do it for them, we sort of lie back and swoon."

"Do we?"

"Metaphorically, I mean. In the end it's sort of less trouble to let the other person take over, force everything, pace, mood, name the goals. But you mustn't, Rebecca."

"No, I won't."

Nellie smoked on the cigarette. ". . . Because then Robert will have taken away from you what he loves now, unless all he loves is his power over you, the reflection of himself."

"Well, hardly, Nellie."

"Don't be insulted, Rebecca, it's just the little dynamic

I always notice with Hugo when he gets back. It's such a struggle to keep the separation when he returns."

"Sure, by then you've had all the separation you can stand. Why 'struggle,' all these words? Don't think like that and it won't be like that." She would have liked to have it out with Nellie, but she had just now lost her hold on their conversation and was off like a dog after a rabbit remembering some sound or movement of Robert's. Anyway, if Nellie's marriage lacked space or required it, Rebecca's life was all too happily taken up with achieving closeness. The commitment she had already made, the closeness would be its reward. And besides that, she was confident that she would be all right, or if not, wrong in a different way, because whatever happened would happen to her and not to Nellie.

"Do you want more coffee?" she asked, "Or do you want a drink?" Rebecca looked at her watch, "Actually, Nellie, I've got to get dressed, it's after twelve now."

"You get dressed," said Nellie, "I'm off. Tell me how lunch goes—Sara and so on. I'm never clear when I speak to Louisa lately whether she's being brave about things or genuinely cheerful."

"I know, it's hard to tell."

"Can't understand why she didn't like England, so suited really."

"Yes," said Rebecca, laughing, holding her kimono closed with one hand and embracing Nellie with the other. "Thanks for all the pre-marital advice. I'll call you later."

"Tell me how she likes the nightie, first reaction."

"Oh, she'll love it. Bye, Nellie, you're a good girl."

"Thanks," said Nellie. They kissed goodbye.

Nellie walked down the steps of Rebecca's apartment building bemused, to say the least, by her exchange with her sister. With what ease she had spoken! But it hadn't been hypocrisy, exactly, this advising on marriage while blithely jeopardizing her own. And not simply because Hugo might find out about Connaly, but because Nellie herself might find herself caught with Connaly, a real person, after all, with whom real feelings might well surface, and after real feelings, who knows what catastrophe. It was all working out badly. Nellie had imagined she was taking Connaly on to redeem her own adolescent past. But in a dishearteningly short space of time, Connaly had triumphed, or rather the present had, and like one of those unhealthily pink and fat cherubs in baroque painting, a tiny tenderness had hovered by the bedside whenever Nellie and Connaly had been together.

But just as it had been foolish to "take on" Connaly for a principle of honor, so it was foolish to think she could simply relinquish him for the sake of the abstraction Marriage or because Sara had shown clearly how much pain was possible when Marriage was destroyed. There was a way of construing, after all, the thing to mean that it was the confessing to, rather than the doing of, the adultery that caused the pain.

And to be truthful, one had to allow some role to the power of desire, to recognize that if Nellie could fall, or begin to slide, for Connaly (already disastrously *had*, for goodness sake), then Ricky could quite understandably, even forgivably, have fallen for this other girl. You had to credit adultery with that—that at least it wasn't acting in cold blood. But there was a people-in-glass-houses aspect to her affair with Connaly, her (and Sara's) gender being the glass house, independent sexual action being the stone. If Nellie was going to be independent of the conventions (her own bloody conventions, her own deadly puritanism, for goodness sake!) she shouldn't be surprised if that independence was to land her up to her neck in foul consequences. But then to preach such high-minded nonsense to Rebecca, that was really asking for it, really inviting the stuff to hit the fan.

Either that, said Nellie, or, since you know very well that Rebecca is lost in her world with Robert and couldn't be more deaf to what you say, you are preaching, Nellie, and with real urgency, to yourself!

ONE NIGHT Nellie had a dream that she was locked in a thick plastic bubble with what appeared to be Connaly, but wasn't quite. Still, the person dressed like Connaly, a tweed jacket over a Lacoste tee-shirt, top-siders and old socks. Her dreaming self had noticed things she hadn't noticed, like the way Connaly wore his socks, with the heel pockets twisted over his ankles. That apart, the dream was nightmarish, because the person had been Connaly in outward form only, in dress and mannerism and accent. In the dream, the person's large pink freckled hands had lumbered about Nellie's body, not gliding smoothly over her skin, but sticking and bumping, mechanically. It seemed to Nellie when she woke that the dream was a warning of what would happen if she went on with this, how she'd be stuck with Connaly, but stuck with a shell of him, the bare spiritless forms of the man. It seemed to her too, rather oddly, that the dream might also have been about Hugo.

It was not yet morning when she woke, and the room was very dark. Nellie heard Connaly's heavy breathing close to her head and felt his weight next to her in the bed. She did not know if they were touching, for she hadn't woken enough to feel the limits of her skin. She

174

was herself merely a night sensation, a dark heaviness, prone to fears and sadness.

She lay awake wishing Hugo were there, wishing it were a long time ago, wishing to be little and rely on her mother and Rebecca. She wanted her mother young and beautiful, and in constant amorous movement, sweeping through her own life like an impregnable optimism; she wanted Mama to be responsible, there in front of her, taking the blows, passing the good news down through the ranks—of battles won and pleasures forthcoming. "Tonight," she would say to Nellie and Rebecca, "we are going to make Sara's birthday cake, but very secretly, in the kitchen, when Sara is asleep." "Now darling," she wanted to hear her mother say, "I really want you to try harder with your Latin," or "I do wish that just once I could walk in here and find your books on the bookshelves and your clothes in the closet, just once, darling, I do wish."

She wanted to live as though these things only were obstacles to happiness and success. She did not want to know about those other obstacles to happiness and success: car crashes, cancers, suicides, breakdowns, sudden losses and gradual realizations. She wanted Hugo as it was five years ago when he would come, wooing and polite, doing his seductive little dance for her, trying to win her, a humorous anecdote, a new aftershave for his darling's pleasure, a film tonight or shall I cook for you? What, Nellie, does your heart desire? Whatever it is, it cannot be more than I can possibly grant. And that had really then been true.

Of course, there had been a bad past too. Bad past was in its present form lying next to Nellie in her dark bed.

175

Bad past had been, as it happened, redeemed a bit by a recent good present. Good, though confused, and morally twisted by Nellie's need to redeem bad present that had once been good past with Hugo. Because it seemed that Hugo was slipping out of her life, like the last blips of an oscilloscope. Was Hugo lost? Was it possible that what she knew was all that she would have of him? Hugo was meant to be hers for the rest of her life. And how long was that? It could be twenty minutes. Some mad, island-dreaming exile, jumped up on jingo-weed could enter that window over there, toes tapping and looking for portables, to find them instead, Nellie and Connaly. Oh, how embarrassing, thought Nellie, to be headlined together, uncovered by the venging hand, Connaly and her, caught bloody-throated in infamy. It was no joke. Nellie looked across to the windows and watched for a while that they did not open.

Her eyes adjusted to the darkness. She could now make out the forms of Connaly's body where it lay under the light cover, could note the impressive rise of his back and shoulders and experience the same sneaking relief she had felt at seventeen when she could watch him asleep, relief at his being asleep. In those days, awake, he seemed to exist only to humiliate her, lumbering and covering and prodding, bruising her with his hard knees, kneading her with his giant hands, forcing the life out of her. Even now, when Connaly's lovemaking was less wildly desperate, more cool, more tender, Nellie's old fear of his brutalizing nature would return, and she would hold back, inappropriately defensive, until his new gentleness convinced her. They had a kind of truce now, for they had managed to let a tenderness emerge from the argument of their lovemak-

176

ing, and this had seemed to redeem the horrors of the past. And there would be a way of continuing, if Nellie would take it, bidding goodbye secretly or officially to Hugo, to accept what it was that Connaly offered. The old love and the true, Connaly had said. He could stay East, he said, work in New York. Nellie should say.

But that was never really on the cards, for Nellie. It was simply an idea whose length she needed to follow to see where her own stopping was.

Connaly slept on Hugo's side of the bed as though he was going to stay forever. Hugo, when he slept, seemed rather self-contained, not so much withdrawn from Nellie as simply untouchable, although of course he wasn't that and it was perfectly easy to wake him, as Nellie used to do, when Hugo would smile before his eyes were open as though the whole thing had been a trick to get Nellie's attention. But Hugo's sleeping expression had a composure that disturbed Nellie, now that she thought about it, and rather longed to see it. All that apparent lack of anxiety in Hugo boded ill, she thought, as she glanced at Connaly, as though Hugo might perfectly happily sleep without her, as he was doing now, alone she presumed, in Dar es Salaam.

Why was it that sleeping with Connaly made her long for Hugo when she knew that by living with Hugo she merely damaged what was there, made everything, it seemed, so much weaker? How then, was it ever redeemable, other than in imagination, in Hugo's absence, in Nellie's night thoughts? In six days' time, or thereabouts, the scheduled return of her husband would end all this rigmarole, either end it or transform it into a giggly and demeaning protraction of what was not quite right anyhow, or right only insofar as it allowed her to reflect—out of action, out of time—on the noble nature of her unapproachable-in-the-reality husband. How could she or anyone living with the person they loved act and feel at the same time, how fight for space and procedure and at the same time contemplate the opponent, how wrangle while worshipping, and how disguise the one for the other? How really love Hugo and not keep that a contest, that word Rebecca so hates, a struggle?

Nellie slid out of bed, slyly so as not to rouse Connaly, nor allow him to move over into her space, and went into the living-room where her cat was sitting among the pillows of the sofa in full territorial possession. Nellie turned on a lamp and picked up a pile of papers beside her on the little table. Out of this pile slipped Sara's postcard on to Nellie's lap, and from there the imperturbable features of Matisse's odalisque addressed her. The space around the courtesan would rest undisturbed, as painted. Inside that space she was happy and desired, desired and not had. But Hugo and Nellie had not left the space between *them* inviolable. Perhaps the ambition was fatal. Perhaps by crossing into each other's space they had sacrificed the vision in their desire to reach it. Like a fairy mirage, each for the other had vanished, leaving Hugo alone, leaving Nellie alone, with their poor mortal selves.

Now, in the last years little by little, each was taking himself, herself back into the little private spheres and canvases. Nellie could admire Hugo, as she did, from afar now, having sacrificed the shared life for a renewed admiration. Or perhaps that was gone too, perhaps Hugo no longer really loved or admired Nellie, and it only appeared so when he spoke of her to his mother or to friends, when a mere habit of voice, habit of affection would take over and others would hear the spark of happiness that once came naturally to his voice when he said her name or spoke of her, the person who had transformed his life, given it value. No longer, it seemed to Nellie. Hugo was probably back where he had been long before he knew Nellie, or perhaps further back, without the hope, because Nellie had failed him, as he had failed her too, failed to change her, to lead her into the light, to let her change.

So now she would leave Hugo, without anything so disruptive as a leaving, but in this cowardly manner— with the sleeping male next door, the old intruder. Or else, not with Connaly, but in even less dramatic form would Nellie leave Hugo, slipping gradually away, year after year until there would be nothing left of them but shadows and appearances, a dim scent, a faint reminding manner of an old and once powerful presence.

How redeem it? How redeem it? Nellie rocked herself, knees under chin, papers cast aside, cat long gone. How, as soon as he comes back, comes into this room, prevent myself from noticing all the unimportant things, like his tan or his greeting or his suitcase taking up space, and full of clothes to be washed? How to notice nothing but the fact that he is here, back from such a long trip away and willing to be with me again?

A sudden thought reached her then and stopped her where she was. But what if Hugo has felt these things too? What if Hugo is not some alien creature invented for Nellie's existence, approachable and leavable like a desti- nation, like any port, but actually a sensation, wrapped in flesh, different only in that wrapping from herself? What if, as the language has it, Hugo and Nellie felt the same?

179

But how could they? They might answer identically that question, "How are you feeling?" and yet still have descended like pearl divers, plunging from similar rocks, down past the caverns, one one way, one the other, through separating waters, among separate sea-life, in separate danger, before climbing out to answer the question.

But if Hugo is the same as I, said Nellie, he may be as unhappy as I, hence as treacherous, possibly, and likewise deceiving. And if he is other than I am, well, there is the treachery too, since his otherness allows him all manner of action against me: he could easily, in short, leave me. Nellie, you ass, he has left. He is away. And as soon as he goes you plow his bed with your highschool lover and torment yourself with thoughts of his leaving you! If only Hugo knew, he *would* leave, he'd be a fool not to. That is just what I mean, Nellie said to herself.

Nellie began now to fix on Hugo as that separate being. More than separate, in the very act of separating himself from her. She began to imagine him on his trip. But she'd been so uncurious. It was hard to remember now exactly why he was going, to stay with whom precisely, which part of the book was he researching? She was so pathetically vague about her husband, no wonder she thought he was slipping away. And now, not with the really flimsy and so pacifying notion of Hugo in the arms of some local temptation, but with the suddenly clear sight of him in a hotel room, air-conditioner buzzing in the background, lurid Safari paintings on the wall, she thought about Hugo, immobile with self-questioning, thinking about himself and Nellie, and whether it was the proper moment to leave.

Nellie lit a cigarette and began to smoke, really only to

make herself a sign of her distress and to punctuate her sense that Hugo might not come back. The thought, a giant night realization, fell with a thump against her breast. She could now see Hugo clearly, lying on his hotel bed with one arm under his head, staring at the ceiling and plagued by guilt and clichés about quick cuts and kindness, wondering whether to phone or write or send a telegram: "My darling, I am staying here a while longer"; "Nellie—it's no good, it just doesn't work"; "Do not expect me, Nellie, I shall not return." Night fears, black certainties.

Nellie got up and paced the room frantically. Where does it come from this certainty and fear of abandonment? She tried to think. Was it from her mother? But Louisa, as far as Nellie knew, had never been left. Yet at that hour of the night it seemed to Nellie that all that constant traffic of her mother's was just a diverting tactic for her fear of it, that Louisa threw them over before being thrown herself. Well, there was Sara. But, said Nellie, Sara is Sara, and Ricky, Ricky, both with private histories, surely. We can't all simply be acting out some hideous biological destiny, disguised more than controlled by an overlay of social mores—thin enough if you think of all those decades of adultery, the years and years and years of it, before it was even called that, the pairing and unpairing, when the women sat and waited and the men came and went, fucking and departing like hundreds of little milkmen down the ages. But perhaps Sara's situation is not only typical, but inescapable. Too late! Too late for Sara, too late for Louisa, oh far too late for Rebecca, and for you too, Nellie. Something's been lost, irrevocably, irretrievably misplaced. You didn't fight nobly enough to keep loving

Hugo. It's gone now, tired and faded and ill, it's crept away. Hugo's telegram will only be the long-overdue announcement of its death.

Tears ran down Nellie's cheek on to her naked legs, scrunched under her now on the sofa. It was true and she mourned. She cried for the dead love and for her cowardice and for the misery of her future alone, and with not the slightest sense of irony that might have come from the presence of Connaly next door. Yet it was correct that Nellie should cry, having slid for years in cowardice and shapeless dreads, reason enough to weep.

The switch that Nellie had touched as she entered the living-room from the long bare-floored hallway was the source of light for several lamps that now shone in the night darkness and gave several areas of the big room a kind of oleographic sanctity. Maternally mourning, for her own dear self as well as the unreturning Hugo, Nellie contemplated these interruptions in the gloaming. Near the large, uncurtained window that faced north, the lamp cast its light on a pale Victorian chair and a low desk at which she now visualized Hugo as he often sat, reading his newspapers, deeply concentrating on stories of war and murder, oblivious to the activity inside the room, whatever that might be: Nellie searching for a sandal, lifting up Hugo's leg or the bottom of his paper to do so, or the cat in its regular pre-prandial panic, when driven by some deep insecurity of its own, it would charge flat-bellied from one end of the room to the other, apparently willing to leap to its death nine floors below, through the very window that framed the light on to Hugo's evening news.

Or, over there, by the long table where a vase had not held fresh flowers since Hugo's departure, Nellie saw her husband wandering, drink in hand, talking backwards over his shoulder to Nellie lying on the sofa, arguing perhaps in that continual argument on six themes which was the sign of their harmony, and which so long as there was no radical change of subject never failed to do as was intended, reassure that all was well inside the kingdom, the boundaries set and well protected, from this understanding to that, thus far and no further.

Nellie got up and went towards the lamp near the window, turning off the light at the base switch. The natural light of the city—if there was any natural light—was becoming stronger, and with it, through the open window, the mysterious morning smell of the city as though after rain. In the early summer the streets gave off a sweet, heavy odor of damp that scented the thin blue light encircling the street lamps and made you feel that even if it hadn't rained in the night, that something else had happened, or would happen, as if by magic, in secret while you slept, simply because it was New York. By such smells and sweet light did the city betray its inhabitants, lulling them into dreams of futures, drugging them against the effects of time, inertias and habituations.

I must do something, said Nellie. But what is it I must do? Telegram Hugo that he must come back? But that would be idiotic. If he's intending to come back, he'll be alarmed, and if not, a telegram from me will hardly change his mind. Well, all right, I must be different if he comes back, nicer. Nicer? What an idea, and that's not it at all. Must what, then? Nellie tried, pushing her forehead on to the cold glass of the window, seeing and not seeing the little dim lights on the streets below, only vaguely taking in the look of the city street, but concentrating all her thoughts on Hugo. Then, thanks to some sudden change of light, or movement of air, Nellie noticed the corner of the building opposite, its size and density and the surface of the stone, and at that moment thought she understood what it was she must do with Hugo—sort of focus on him, put him in a line of sight, recognize him and at the same time recognize the distance between them. She must acknowledge the space between them and their separateness and then she must cast away that distance and, without owning or disarming or trespassing, love him. If I love Hugo, said Nellie, it is because he is over there, not here where I am. Where I am, that is me. He is over there and I am over here, accept that distance as proper space, and then cross it. Yes, said Nellie, that is it. Well, easily said. The crossing of all that space takes nerve. Nellie sighed and returned to the couch. The cat, excited by the prospect of an unscheduled early breakfast, purred and rubbed against Nellie's legs. "Go away," she said out loud to the cat. She was unhappy again. Others, cats, Connaly next door, laden with sleep and his own otherness, his will that also had to be fed in the morning.

Connaly, miraculously, remained asleep as Nellie bathed, dressed and left early for work. It surprised her that this was so and pleased her, rather as if she were her old seventeen-year-old self having escaped his demands, and not herself who enjoyed sex with Connaly and had felt well and happy since he'd come to stay with her.

At lunchtime Connaly phoned Nellie at her office to say he was going to be late back and wanted to take her out to dinner. He said, too, that there had been a telegram that morning, but he'd not opened it and would bring it with him tonight. Was that OK? Yes, she said, that was all right; and again she felt the sensation of escape—not of Hugo, announcing his decision to stay in Africa, but of Connaly who might have had, had he opened the cable, rather more information about Nellie and perhaps about their future than Nellie would have liked.

In the afternoon, as Nellie worked on her catalog, Louisa telephoned to thank her for her birthday present. "You get things right, my darling," her mother said, "even when late." It seemed too, Louisa said, that Sara was showing signs of improvement.

"What signs, Mama?" said Nellie.

"What? Well, she looks a bit better; she's combing her hair again, and this is, yes, the tenth morning that she's been up more or less decently—I mean before eleven."

"Yes?" said Nellie, "anything else?"

"Well, just that really," said Louisa, "but if you'd been watching around here as I have—no reproach, Nellie, you understand—you'd be grateful for such indications as these. I may be kidding myself," said Louisa, sounding very pleased, "but I don't think so. She is not yet singing in the shower, but she seems rather regularly to be taking them, and she is combing her hair. Or so it appears."

Well, Sara was going on; perhaps, thought Nellie, the little yellow Western Union envelope flapping at the edge of her consciousness, going on was all that mattered, a little fortitude, a little cheer. Thus she wrote dates and centimeters pertaining to her artists, picturing them in overalls, down at the Cedar, tanking up, really quite liking it all, authenticity and agony, that "struggle," whose peripheries they knew and over whose edges they sometimes crawled to look, taking their brushes with them, and some tough talk, but not much else.

Nellie left the office that evening with a sense that she should be grateful for this job, for so much continuity, for the fact that there was one aspect of her life for which she had competence, one place that would be safe, relatively speaking, from sudden swings of fate, sudden depletions of character. In such a job she could perform if necessary as an empty shell, for weeks on end. And far from resenting this, she felt for the first time something like the strived-for workers' gratitude. Telegram or no, her little desk, clean and steely, dusted by equally safe (more or less) employees, would be there for her tomorrow. For such continuity she gave thanks, greeting in genuine comrade-ship the receptionist at the elevator doors, and she in turn was bolstered by that lady's truism: "See you tomorrow."

But once inside the elevator, Nellie sensed again that she was alone. Descending slowly to the street, she felt herself held by a sudden conviction: I am going to get hurt. My calm and happy existence is about to be turned on its head. What is more, said Nellie, listening to herself as though not knowing what was coming next, it is all my fault. I have simply, as with my smoking, ignored the warnings too long. And even if it is not this time, it will be soon; there is an ice wall or a plastic bubble, or what-ever it is between myself and my world, myself and Hugo. It is me shutting him out, or him shutting me. I can see him on the other side, smiling, but God knows not im-mortal, and he won't sit out there forever. And with him and really reachable only after I reach him, are all the things of my world: trees and shoes and dogs and Gorky and Pollock, all lovable and not properly loved. And why? Because I can't break through, out of fear. But of what? Of being in the precise state I describe, because, perhaps, if I break the glass, I must first admit that it is there. But that's ridiculous, Nellie was almost shouting to herself inside the slow elevator. Well, she answered, rather sulkily, perhaps it's Hugo's fault too; perhaps the fear is of the consequences of that wall's being broken, and then having to—but must it be inevitable?—return to my place behind it.

Out on the street the New Yorkers were making their way home, looking for cabs, running for buses, offering each other drinks or else head down rapt in thoughts of dinners, children, wives, mistresses, bosses or secretaries, wrapped by these thoughts as separate bundles moving through space, rather as cows move wrapped in flies. Among these preoccupied walkers, and like them, not noticing the weather or street exchanges, tenth-story windows or manhole covers, limping pigeons or cigarette papers, was Nellie on her way home and thinking about Hugo. Worse, she was not even really thinking about Hugo but of how she would cope if they were to divorce. As though tapping her knees with a little rubber hammer, she questioned her state to see if she was in good shape for catastrophe, tested her income to figure what sort of place she would live in, tested her age and her looks. I'll be too old for children next time (next time! Already, Nellie, what a wretched little pragmatist, Louisa's daughter all right). Who would befriend her in her misery? Rebecca and perhaps Louisa. Who would be impatient with her? Robert and Connaly. Connaly? He'd be only too delighted to step in and repossess.

Oh shit, said Nellie, all this speculation is unnerving, almost exciting, a coming test, a crisis. But then, suddenly realizing what it might all actually mean in terms of

Hugo's disappearance, she came to a stop suddenly in the middle of the street and allowed herself to take a blow of panic. Nellie walked on until she reached the corner, where waiting to cross, she allowed herself the thought again, took another blow, carefully measuring what she could handle, cautious about what she would endure, almost splitting herself in two in anticipatory suffering: the coping, impartial guide and witness, and the sorrowful, victim self.

And all the while this was going on, Nellie was careful not to betray the smallest hint of anguish, but to cross the street when the others did, to halt with them at the lights, to walk uptown on the outside of the street, to anticipate oncoming pedestrians and adjust her speed to theirs, stepping aside when necessary, smiling when provoked, discouraging conversation and sexual interest and managing to look to the outside world as though she hadn't a thought in her head, just another happy, weary working girl, on her way home.

But that wouldn't do, because coming towards her in every crowd was the evidence of similar strain and camouflage: lips moving in silent speech, eyes that shifted or stared dead ahead, arms moving badly with the rest of the body, bad toupees, bad makeup, tight jackets with short sleeves, the wrong styles on the wrong people, the wrong shapes for the wrong ages, signals everywhere that parts and wholes did not, could not fit.

"And I," said Nellie, "am about to be shunted one step further along this route. Further and further away from the world, because I have not accepted the world as it is. I made contact all right, but with the wrong party. And unless I get that right, always supposing it is just in time

188

and not too late, I also will be regarded as someone 'out of things.' I might be able to fake it for a while, but I'll know and I'll scare myself."

And soon, Nellie was beside herself, holding her own hand in self-pity.

It was about seven when Nellie got off the cross-town bus and walked along Central Park West towards her soon-to-be-broken home, and about seven-thirty when she crossed the hall and went to lie down on her bed. The room had been tidied by Connaly before he'd left, and the bed had been made, or rather the sheets and blanket had been pulled lumpily upwards, enough to give the impression of a new purposeful presence in the place. It was curious how with Hugo Nellie always noticed the disorder of a tie across the chair, bits of shaved beard in the sink, as though all signs of his living were a violation of some pristine order, some idealizing sensibility of hers; yet in the case of a real intruder and quite a disruptive one— Connaly lived as though forever trailed by bending and dusting domestics—she had no sense of grievance, simply a more or less cheerful capitulation to their difference and a mild curiosity about the likely state of his own apartment. She tried to remember what it had been like to share a hotel room with Connaly, all those years ago, and assumed from her vagueness that it was not then part of one's consciousness of cohabitation: mess, order. In those days there were more important problems of living together to be worked through.

Well, was it really that or the *femme de chambre?* And if not, if the former, was it true then that Hugo and Nellie's life together existed on the formalest, formalist level—and did that preclude other levels? Was their orderliness a sign

189

of harmony or was it a code meant to fool? And if so, who was being fooled?

The kind of urgency with which, in the early hours of the morning, Nellie had regarded various corners of her home had vanished, and in the flat evening light that cast itself into the place, Nellie regarded her surroundings with detachment. The thought of dividing books and records seemed too abysmal, perhaps in the event she would just leave everything, start again. What about the cat? What about her set of Trollope? It was no good. For it was true that everything she was now had in some measure been made, altered by the existence of such things: books, drawings, music, other people's journeys. The illusion of the free future demanded she cut with such signs of the past, falsifying history by denying it, substituting for a notion of predestination a notion of grace.

Among the bookshelves in front of her were her books, a history of the questions she'd asked of novels, art books, poetry, mostly the same question asked about what was out there and how to join it. Hugo's books, on the other hand, asked and answered the question differently, how the world worked in its more public manifestations, its population cycles and agroeconomics, gold markets and military struggles, industrial relations and urban planning. It would not be difficult to separate the books: Nellie's were all about things that could matter only if the subjects of Hugo's books allowed them to. But one bubbling up of war or famine at the right time and place and all talk of art and love and spiritual ambition would seem like so much fabling—allegories to pacify children, tales to coax them into their dreams of life.

In the bedroom Nellie took off her clothes and dropped

190

them on the Connaly-made bed. In the bathroom she turned on the shower, happy to feel the cold shower handles and the hot water on her head and spine. At the same time she marveled at the almost careless manner in which she performed these things—undressing, washing, turning taps on and off, regulating hot and cold, as though someone else and not she were on the verge of some awful piece of fortune.

But it was she, wasn't it, here, at thirty, precisely where she'd engineered herself not to be. About to be left. Alone. Abandoned. About to be dropped at the foot of that terrible mountain, over which she would have to climb to recover. About to start the pathetic little hacking away at the shrubs at the bottom, throwing up the pick, tying ropes, whatever it was you did, in full sweat and not looking down for a long long time until you got to the peak or the other side or—to mix again her metaphor and thereby reconvince herself of her uneasy grasp of *such* realities—to *terra firma*. And even then there would be no guarantees. For hadn't Rebecca ended after just such a long and bruising climb with the—to Nellie—less than desirable Robert? And wasn't Sara even now refusing to acknowledge the mountain in front of her, but settling for perdition on the lower slopes? And hadn't Nellie been with Hugo there where she was aiming at and still not been able to plant her little flag and say with conviction Here I Stand, or whatever it was that was said in those circumstances? Yes, yes, yes, Nellie, yes to it all.

"Well, Nellie," said Nellie to herself, this time out loud and looking in the mirror to take off the last traces of the day's makeup with the corner of a towel, "here you are, more or less where you were before, much older and no smarter, about to go out for the evening, a single girl with a single purpose which is to lose that sense of being All Alone. But you know, don't you, that that is the real habitat for everyone: All Alone, and not only All Alone, but in the dark as well."

And this thought made her almost cheerful so that she put on a red silk sheath and gold earrings, and rigid with bravado, added kohl to her eyelids and color to her cheeks, Shalimar to the back of her neck.

"Well, off you go," she said to her image in the mirror, as though to the hero of an RAF film, "and good luck."

Nellie's sense of being a single girl out on a date with a potential lover did not last long enough to get her inside the restaurant doors and into the banquette where Connaly had seated himself, besuited and "cleaned up" to wait for her. For one thing the potential lover was Connaly and for another, she had a sudden notion that she might very well be recognized here by an acquaintance of hers or Hugo's. In that case it would be made clear by her dress as much as her proximity to Connaly on the banquette— already with one arm over her shoulder in greeting (didn't he know that the point of these adjacent seatings was titillation, thigh to thigh, as above the table line the artichoke vinaigrette sank into indifferent faces, and not simply for easier, sloppier access?)—that this was a *dîner d'amour*, as it was called by the rather more practiced French.

Nellie separated herself slightly from Connaly, who laughed, and looked cautiously about her in the restaurant. Various diners were staring at them, it was true, but as far as Nellie could make out, none known to herself or

Hugo. Goodness, was she forever going to worry about appearances and go on thinking she were Hugo's property, or would she now, finally, begin to acknowledge that she was, for better or for worse, in sickness or in health, her own person?

"Connaly, let go of my arm," she said, as unirritably as she could make it sound, "and can I please have a drink?" This was a long way from the demure hypocrite of their first meeting, and as Nellie noticed herself, she was scornful.

"Why do you always say *no* to me?" Connaly asked as he removed his arm. But he asked almost out of intellectual curiosity, and there was no reproach in it.

Nellie looked at him. "Do I?" she said. "Well, it's pretty public. Can I have a drink?"

"And you always want the conversation on your terms, and the action to follow your plans—like now, you want to change the subject and you want a drink, when you want it. Now why is that?"

"I don't know," said Nellie, trying not to let the annoyance into her voice. "Maybe you're wrong. Maybe you only think so. Maybe it's because you always want to win. If I can't have a drink, may I at least have a sip of yours?" She smiled.

"And what," said Connaly, smiling back, "if I say no?"

Nellie put her hand up to call the waiter. He looked surprised and slightly offended, but that, as Nellie knew, was how, acting as a waiter, he was meant to look. She ordered her drink.

"See," said Connaly, "you don't need me, do you?"

"What is this all about?" Nellie asked him.

"You're a very independent lady, that's all. Headstrong, I would say. A real loner."

At the last word, Nellie sat up. "Not at all," she said, "I don't like being bullied, that's all."

"Oh, is that all it is?" Connaly asked. "Well, I won't bully you much longer. I'm off Sunday."

"Off?" Nellie said.

"Yes, isn't that how you say it? Off? I'm off, I was on, but now I'm off. I'll leave you in peace."

"Why?" Nellie was distraught. For a moment she thought Connaly was punishing her for ordering her own drink.

"But I thought," she said to Connaly.

"Yes?" He smiled slowly.

"That you were happy." She was faltering now, not at all tough. Her other self—rejected.

"Happy with what you choose to give me of yourself? Well, yes, I suppose I was happy, but then I'm usually pretty happy," he said to her. "However, just speaking off the top of my head—here's your telegram, by the way—I would say there's no point my sticking around this particular situation, since your heart, it seems, is otherwise engaged, and as for the rest, the rest I can get elsewhere. Maybe not so nice [Nellie smiled a little sourly at his gallantry] but good enough, considering what I'm looking for doesn't come with it."

"Which is?" said Nellie, curious. She had the telegram in her hand, not opening it.

"Some sort of commitment to me, to the fact that I'm here."

"But," said Nellie, outraged, "I am married." Her voice carried. A woman at a neighboring table smiled in condescension at Nellie, a smile that said, "Oh *that* objection, honey, that'll go, just give it time."

Nellie looked at Connaly. She was stuck and confused. *She* was being put in the philanderer's role; *she* was being accused of having misled and abused the kind heart and willing loins of her companion. Almost absent-mindedly she put the telegram in her pocket.

"Listen, my old friend," said Connaly with lowered voice, "that is precisely the trouble. You *are* married and you should stay that way. You've been sweet and nice to me, but there's nothing more than love for old times' sake there. Stick to Hugh or Hugo or whatever his name is, and put your heart in it."

"Old times' sake," said Nellie. "Are you kidding? Do you have any idea what those old times consisted of? You forcing me, you shouting at me, you beating me up."

"I never beat you up," said Connaly, laughing. The lady at the next table was now quite unselfconsciously listening, no longer even chewing.

"Yes. You rowed me out to that awful island once, off the summer place, you remember? And marooned there on that fucking, condom-littered dumping ground, you practically raped me. You hit me. It was revolting, revolting. Surely you haven't forgotten. Or did you always hit girls in those days?"

"No. And I don't remember it. But I would imagine that if I hit you on that particular day it was because you were asking for it."

"Oh," said Nellie furious. She felt for her telegram, but left it again immediately. No comfort there.

"Yes, asking for it—once again and characteristically refusing, saying no, wanting it all your own way, wanting to call all the shots, just like now. It's you, Nellie, who are boorish, not me, it's you who want to override everyone's will, you—in your ladylike way, Nellie, are the bully."

"Oh fuck you," said Nellie.

"And you'd do that too if you could."

"Oh fuck you," said Nellie, at a sudden loss for words. And at the same time as Nellie loathed Connaly she was thinking (1) He is right, because what I hate most about this particular scene is the fact of his triumph now, his successful humiliation of me and his decision to go off—it was for me to have told him to go and he should have waited; and (2) It's not too late, I can have him still. If I've lost Hugo, I can't afford to lose him. Repair it, take him home, offer him a loving future.

But she said, "Listen, Connaly, that may have been the way in the past. I was young, you were like a steamroller. I had to keep something apart or I would have died under your weight."

Connaly's brows raised, in mockery of the image. Nellie ignored him, but not the couple at the next table, whose cutlery was now down, to make less noise, the better to hear what was being said.

"But this time," she said, "this time surely [but she refused to flirt, she was simply asking out of ignorance], surely I gave something up, gave you something?"

"Listen to the way you talk," said Connaly, good-natured but serious. "It's not giving stuff up, giving something away, it's the opposite. You don't know what fucking loving is."

"What is it?" said Nellie. "What is it?"

"It's bringing yourself to the party, it's being with the other person, being there, not being separate. You always

196

stay alone, off by yourself at your own separate cocktail party. What are you afraid of?"

"Of being alone."

"That's fucking ridiculous," said Connaly. "You do it."

"I don't know," said Nellie, "maybe I do."

Connaly grabbed her hand with unmistakable aggression. Nellie winced; she thought for a moment he was going to plead for himself.

"Here's my hand," he said. "It's warm isn't it? It's attached to a warm body. You're not out there in space on your own little orbit, you're sitting here in this restaurant connected by your skin to me and by the talk to me and by your hunger to me and by our coexistence at the same exact time—" he looked at his watch "—9.22 in New York City, on Wednesday June 25, 1981, fifty years before we shall be connected only by the fact that we are dead and once lived and once were together on the same planet, once on the Atlantic, once in England, once in Paris, once in New York, and once, if you like, on Pine Point Island, where the only way I could connect with you, touch you, reach you was by trying to smash your face in [Nellie laughed] because you wouldn't let me love you, like you won't let me now. Which is OK and I'll go, just as long as you don't end up with no one else, and worse, a conviction that because you feel all alone that there is no one else out there."

"Yes," Nellie said after a while. "But it's hard."

"Sure," said Connaly, "but you've gotta do it. Otherwise," he made a gesture with his hand across his throat and picked up his menu. "I want a steak," he said. "What do you want?"

. . . .

197

Nellie got back to her apartment around eleven, grateful that Connaly was spending this night in his fairly unused hotel room, and tried to understand the implications of being thus twice left. She had a sort of fatigue about the whole thing and a sense that there was going to be a long run on her energy in the weeks to come, and on sanity and courage. She had carried her telegram all the way home without opening it, and now took it, together with a pack of cigarettes and matches from the restaurant, across the hall to the living-room sofa. Nellie took off her shoes and dragged the large ashtray on to her lap, lit a cigarette and opened the yellow envelope. For a second the words popped and jumped around. Then she read:

ARRIVING MONDAY JUNE 30 20 HOURS HUGO

No love, no message, just that announcement, rather bare in the allotted space, rather military. At first Nellie assumed that something had been left out by the wire service, then she assumed that Hugo was going to make his announcement in person. Finally, she understood that Hugo was simply coming back.

But this time she also knew that he would be back only for a while, whether that would be one week or fifty years, and that he could only be with her temporarily.

A visit, Hugo was coming to visit her, Nellie. She could welcome him or she could wish him elsewhere, it was up to her. But his return was a kind of first step, in answer to which she, if she wished to be with him, must come back too.

Alone in bed, Nellie slept long and deeply, an unaccompanied sleep from which she woke groggily around nine o'clock. She was still inside a dream, but a kind of daydream through which she saw the light of the sun through the venetian blinds, and the shape of the chair back in front of the window. Beyond these things, or in front of them, she saw a pale yellow beach on a sunny summer afternoon, late, when the shadows were long and a wind stirred the beach grasses. She heard in her reverie men's voices and the soft sound of the ocean. Then she saw the figures on the beach, called back from the dead for this late afternoon game on the sand at Louse Point: Pollock with his recent beard and heavy head, one paw wrapped around a can of beer, shouting from first base to David Smith, rubbing the softball over his large chest at second. And Smith was laughing at Rothko in outfield because he'd missed a catch. And watching all this, not playing, was Bill de Kooning, and with him, not entirely relaxed, the tall loping figure of Arshile Gorky. Nellie was there too, in striped tee-shirt and jeans, and in outfield, Hugo, she thought, even Louisa under her sunglasses, and Sara and Rebecca, even Robert. Overseeing all of this, a little impatient for the game to start, was the man behind Franz Kline at home plate, wearing his umpire's hat, a short cigar between his teeth, eyes glinting in the sun, organizing the whole thing and waiting—Bateman.

When he had everyone's attention, he held it for a moment and then shouted, "OK, boys, you know what we're here for. Play ball."

JANET HOBHOUSE was born in 1948 in New York City, where she lived until she went to England at the age of sixteen. She read English at Oxford University and returned to New York in 1971, when she began to write about art. In 1975 she published *Everybody Who Was Anybody: A Biography of Gertrude Stein;* in 1988, *The Bride Stripped Bare: The Artist and the Female Nude in the Twentieth Century.* She is also the author of four novels, including *The Furies.*

Ms. Hobhouse was a contributing editor of *ARTnews* and a fellow of the New York Institute for the Humanities. She wrote on theater for *Vogue.* Janet Hobhouse died in 1991.